MAYWOOD PUBLIC LIBRARY

1312 00142 6982

P9-CRW-882

On the Edge of Popularity

*A young adult
novel by
Lauren Lee*

Library of Congress
Cataloging-in-Publication Data

Lee, Lauren
Stella: On the Edge of Popularity/Lauren Lee–1st ed.
       p.   cm.

Summary:
Hoping to be accepted by a popular seventh grade
clique, a Korean American girl is embarrassed by her
family's heritage–until a series of events gives her a
better sense of who she is.

ISBN No. 1-879965-08-9 : $10.95
1. Korean Americans — Fiction.
2. Schools— Fiction.
3. Identity—Fiction.
4. Family life—Fiction.
I. Title

PZ7.L51284St   1994
[Fic]—dc20

                        93-43917
                          CIP
                          AC

This is a New Book, Written and Illustrated
Especially for Polychrome Books
First Edition, May 1994

Copyright © 1994 By Polychrome Publishing
Corporation. All rights reserved. Except for short
excerpts for review purposes, no part of this book
may be reproduced or transmitted in any form by
any means, electronic or mechanical, including
photocopying, without permission in writing from
the Publisher.

All characters in this book are fictitious, and any
resemblance to actual persons living or dead is
coincidental.

Designed, produced and published by
Polychrome Publishing Corporation
4509 North Francisco Avenue
Chicago, Illinois 60625-3808
(312) 478-4455 Fax: (312) 478-0786

Editorial Director, Sandra S. Yamate
Art Director, Heather Mark Chen
Production Coordinator, Brian M. Witkowski

Printed in Hong Kong
10 9 8 7 6 5 4 3 2 1

ISBN 1-879965-08-9

stella *On the Edge of Popularity*

Dedicated to my father,
who nurtured my free mind,
and my father-in-law,
who provided me
with free time.

❦

Author's Note

The effort, support, and forbearance of many people have helped to make *Stella* a reality. A writer's first book is as much a challenge of confidence as of skill. I'd like to try and acknowledge those who contributed.

Justine Stewart, Daisy Barrios, Sarah Sohn, Margaret Breffeilh, and Samiksha Patel informed me about being twelve years old, being a young person of color, or being Korean American.

Other helpful readers included friends and family. Thanks to my friends, Anne Westerberg and Lorijo Metz. My former high school English teacher, Michael Benedict, propelled the work forward with his penetrating questions. Christine Bahn gave professional advice throughout, and sister-in-law Elizabeth Lee raised the red flag appropriately. Finally, Nancy Williams illuminated some important grammatical rules and lent a kind ear.

For research, I drew of course upon my own experiences as a teacher and as a member of the Korean American community, but memories need refreshing. The staff of Lincoln Hall Middle School in Lincolnwood, Illinois, was helpful. Anita Battaglia staged relevant discussions for me. Wendy Kotrba invited me to the spelling bee, and Pat Ulmer found time to have students read a draft of the manuscript. Dr. Mary Lou Johns, the principal, allowed me to impinge on her school's resources and time. Karen Laner of Chiaravalle Montessori School in Evanston, Illinois found Margaret for me. Mrs. Kwon Ok Chon of Howard Shirt and Dry Cleaners and Mrs. Pio Park of Weslun Cleaners allowed me to poke around in their places of business.

Other writers gave of their insight and time. The community at the Off-Campus Writer's Workshop has been interested and supportive. Visiting authors Marion Markham, Stella Pevsner, and Dorothy Haas responded cogently to portions of the manuscript. Mary Collins, my writing partner, spent many hours in the Cafe Attitude pointing out inconsistencies. The laughter was especially helpful, Mary.

We are extremely fortunate in having many loving hands reaching out to our daughter, Deirdre Hee Sook Lee, so I could have free time to write. My in-laws, Solomon and Theresa Lee, provided Deirdre a universe of love and unbridled delight. Notably, Solomon Lee came over every Thursday morning, enabling me to attend writer's group and get this book started.

Your devotion and Christian wisdom are unparalleled, Abpanim. Ellen Rodriguez and the Oliver-Takadas (especially Anna-Tarzana) provided a nurturing and welcoming place for Deirdre as well. Mi Ran Yoon provided a sisterly friendship to me and last-minute care to Deirdre in the deadline crunch, despite having a new child to care for. Jin Park provided stellar childcare, valuable advice, and a friendly ear, all on a daily basis.

My father Paul Eck and his wonderful wife, Susan Robson Eck, indulged my interminable phone calls while I struggled forward. Maria Sandora-Meeder of Oppenheimer Wolff & Donnelly did much the same, as well as providing technical assistance (given, as usual, generously and much beyond the call of duty). The communities at St. Luke's Episcopal Church and the Galter Life Center listened kindly at all times.

Sandra Yamate asked that such a book be written, gave excellent advice throughout its composition, and responded to it quickly and positively. Sandra, your encouragement made all the difference in the world. This book would not have been written without you.

Finally, there are things I can never adequately put into words. John Yo-Hwan Eck Lee elucidated Stella's outlook for me, sacrificed throughout the writing process, and stayed up late to edit. Deirdre Hee Sook Lee has been a terrific little girl despite my lapses in effective parenting. Danny Dog remained sweet and protective even when left without attention or walks for days at a time. Thanks.

Chapter 1

Grandmother and Kim Chee

Stella Sung Ok Kim was in a good mood on Friday; that is, she was until she smelled the kim chee. Its sharp, rich odor hit her like a wall as she walked in the front door of their split-level house that afternoon, but it was nothing compared to her Grandmother. Grandmother made Stella's life hard: making Stella work, criticizing her clothes, and, worst of all, favoring Stella's brothers. And this kim chee. . . It was embarrassing.

Everyone else eats normal food like pizza, Stella thought as she pulled off her blue winter coat and hung it in the closet. She looked around for a moment, not knowing what to do. She often felt confused when she came home. She sat down on the foyer's linoleum tile, struggled to take off her boots, and thought for a moment. Then she looked at the boots. They were pink and wore a designer stamp, the same as Eileen's. Stella's mind seemed to clear. She touched her hair, styled like

Eileen's, too. Stella smiled.

Stella lifted her soft, rounded nose in the air to inhale the kim chee's changing smell. It seemed buttery and soft now. Suddenly, as if a food could change personalities, its odor turned red-hot and garlicky and slapped her in the face, grabbing her attention. It was time to pass through the wall of kim chee smell and enter the kitchen.

Grandmother stood with her back to the door, stirring the bright-red marinated cabbage in a pan. "Set the table," said Grandmother in Korean.

Stella shook her head. It was only four o'clock. There was plenty of time, she thought. She stepped to the side to look for a snack.

"You should wear your hair differently," Grandmother continued, "you look too American these days." Stella's hands flew up to her soft dark hair, pulled back in a complicated braid. Stella ducked into the pantry. She took a chocolate muffin out of a box and perched on a stool behind her Grandmother. She tried to eat quickly, without letting the plastic wrapper crinkle.

"You'll spoil your dinner," said her grandmother, without looking up from her cooking. Stella shoved the rest into her mouth, not noticing the soft brown crumbs tumbling onto the shiny tiled floor. She wouldn't say anything, although she realized that Grandmother always said what she thought. Stella wondered what would happen if she did that. She opened her narrow, childlike mouth to speak but then closed it. She slid down from the stool and walked silently toward the silverware drawer, next to the stove.

Stella and her Grandmother were the same height. Her brown-black eyes glanced repeatedly at the older woman, whose thick gray hair pulled the skin tight at her temples, crossed by pink-swirled plastic glass frames resting on a little nose. She ignored Stella's looks, like she ignored the spitting sesame oil biting her skin and smearing her thick plastic lenses. Stella wondered why her Grandmother ignored her.

When the telephone rang, Stella dropped her handful of chopsticks and forks on the table and ran out of the kitchen. She hoped it would be Eileen. They had been best friends until last year. Now Eileen was really popular and Stella . . . Stella didn't know what she was. "Oh, hi, Rachel." Stella's shoulders slumped.

Rachel was Stella's standby friend. Although they studied together sometimes, hanging out with her was too much . . . Rachel never got invited to Eileen's parties. "No, I'm busy on Saturdays," she glanced stiffly at the clock, not wanting to say more. Then Rachel captured her attention.

"Compete in the spelling bee?" A little smile softened her heart-shaped face, and her straight, small white teeth glistened. "Do you really think I could win?" She imagined becoming a winner, but . . .

"No, I can't," she said resignedly, "because Eileen is going to win." Eileen's birthday party was the first weekend in May. Stella wasn't stupid enough to risk not being invited. All the popular kids went.

Stella glanced toward the kitchen, lowered her voice, and scrunched into the stairwell. Maybe Grandmother wouldn't miss her. "Yes, he was asleep again. Jesse's so weird, but he's so cute. It's not fair that he never studies. I can't believe that he sleeps with his eyes open." She scrunched up her shoulders and giggled, hidden slightly by the stairs.

Suddenly, Stella's Grandmother slapped her on the hand.

"Cut off the phone!" she whispered harshly to Stella and turned back to the kitchen. Then Grandmother turned around and added, louder this time, "Finish what you start!" With a shaky hand, Stella covered the phone as she watched her Grandmother stalk back to the kitchen. She stood up.

"I'm sorry, Rachel. I have to go." She returned to the kitchen where her Grandmother stood over the cutting board, shaking her head.

"All you do is waste time," the old woman said as she chopped scallions and hot peppers with hands that moved like air. Stella heard the sharp, insistent sound of a thousand little hits accompanying her Grandmother's voice and the pops of the exploding oil. "At least finish your job before you go off and play." Stella finished setting the kitchen table and then she set another in the dining room, for her parents. In the dining room, Stella set out the unchipped plates and carefully-folded napkins deliberately, so that her parents would feel at peace when they returned from the store. She brushed the seat of her mother's chair.

The telephone's ring jarred Stella back into awareness. She tiptoed into the hallway and picked up the receiver. She prepared to take a message.

"Oh, Eileen!" She clenched her teeth in excitement. As she peeked into the kitchen and started to creep up the stairs, the front door burst open. Frankie flung his books on the floor and turned to Albert. "You idiot!" The noise startled Grandmother, who turned to watch.

Stella hissed, "Shut up, Frankie!" Albert pushed the smaller boy away, grabbed their dirty soccer ball, and faked throwing it at Frankie's head. Frustrated, Frankie turned on his sister.

"Smella!" he called in falsetto, "Is that mean Eileen?"

Covering the phone desperately, her lips pursed, Stella hissed, "Shut up, Frankie."

Frankie grinned like an elf and watched her. When Stella lifted her hand to apologize to Eileen, he shrieked into the receiver, "Mean Eileen who thinks she's a queeeen!" Stella lunged at him, her face white with fear.

"No, it's nothing, Eye- I mean, Eileen . . . No, it's not more important than . . ." She looked pleadingly at Albert.

"I'll race you for the remote!" said Albert. Frankie yelped and raced down the few steps to the rec room, knocking Stella against the wall.

"Yes, you looked great today . . ." Her friend interrupted, and Stella's small square jaw clenched. "Jesse probably does like you," she began biting her nails. "Rachel told me that he stands in the bookstore reading books at the mall. Maybe you can . . ." This time, Stella smiled at the interruption.

"Shopping? Today to see Jesse?"

"Oh," her shoulders slumped, "you and Amanda. And you need the math." Her heart sank, and her stomach twisted and turned. She remembered that Eileen and Amanda were going away for the weekend, that Eileen wouldn't have any time to do the math homework or to prepare for Monday's test. She wondered why Eileen was becoming best friends with Amanda. It seemed impossible to make everything right again, but she could try.

"By what time?" She looked over at her Grandmother, who didn't seem to mind her talking this time. In fact, if she didn't know better, Stella would think she was listening. Never mind, she told herself. Stella's mind raced as she calculated. . . if she dried the dishes fast, didn't help her brothers, worked on her math and didn't spend time with her mother later, then maybe . . .

"Okay, I can have them by eight." Her Grandmother added

cubed tofu into the hot kim chee stew. Stella punched her stomach, so that she wouldn't notice the ache. She looked at the receiver. The dial tone hummed.

"Goodbye." She hung up. Her Grandmother shook her head. Stella told herself that it wasn't possible for Grandmother to understand. As Stella stood thinking, the dramatic sounds of honking horns and shouting men floated up the stairs.

Usually, the boys played soccer until dinner, but today a cold, wet rain had begun to fall, so they came inside to watch T.V. Stella needed to distract herself, so she picked up their coats and put away their boots. The kim chee stew smelled finished. It was time to tell the boys to get ready for dinner. She skillfully kicked the wet soccer ball down the stairs.

In the paneled room, the boys lay sprawled in their seats. Albert watched Stella, but Frankie ignored her. She kicked the ball at Frankie, who didn't flinch. "Get up, lazy bums," she said, "you know it's time to eat." Her hands on her hips, she glared at Frankie. "Thanks for embarrassing me, Frankie." Sensing her anger, Albert swung his big feet to the floor.

"Sung Ok!" yelled her Grandmother, "It's time to eat!"

Frankie wrinkled his nose, rolled his eyes, and sank further into the couch, curling up and holding his skinny knees. Albert looked at Stella with his soft brown eyes.

"Frankie! Get up! Who do you think you are?"

The rice cooker closed — a little click with a gulp of air — as if calling Stella to attention, but Frankie gazed at the T.V. as if hypnotized.

Grandmother's voice sounded more irritated. "Sung Ok! Quit watching T.V.! Do your duty!"

Then something hit her arm, and she balled her fist, ready to swing.

Frankie, snuggled in his seat, hung one arm over the side, clutching another pillow to throw. When Albert laughed, Stella looked toward the sound, and another pillow walloped her in the head.

"Hey!" The three converged dragging pillows, beating each other and howling with laughter. Stella felt a huge relief as she swung the heavy pillows at her brothers.

"There is no dignity in this house!" Grandmother stood at the bottom of the stairs holding a dripping spatula.

"Brothers must be shown a good example!" Stella's stomach sank, and she slowly lowered her pillow to her waist, clutching it like a shield, but it was too late. Grandmother had already left.

Blinking back her tears, she asked Albert, "Why are you always such a baby? Why don't you help me sometimes?" In single file, the three Kim children walked upstairs to eat.

While Grandmother served the meal, Stella noticed the older woman lifting a small piece of marinated beef to her mouth. Before she took a bite, the chopsticks paused in the air and she put the beef on the children's serving plate instead. Grandmother then reached into the stew pan with her chopsticks and took out a broken piece of tofu. Stella couldn't understand what her Grandmother was doing.

❦

After dinner, Stella sat at the kitchen table flipping through her math book. She rested her chin on her hand and stared at the blank white wall. Her parents were still at the dry cleaning shop, working another fourteen-hour day. Tomorrow would be Saturday, and they would at least close the store earlier. Stella would also help out at the store. Stella wondered why it had to be so hard for her parents.

"Concentrate! Maybe you should go upstairs!" said Grandmother, laying the damp pink dishcloth on the counter. Ducking her head, Stella turned the pages in the chapter on fractions.

Over Stella's shoulder the oven light shone dimly. When her Grandmother walked up from the laundry room she stood behind Stella, watching her intently. Every time a car door slammed, Stella's head jerked away from her books and toward the door. She was dreaming of the time when her mother had been home all afternoon, taking care of Stella and letting her play. Her Grandmother put on a pot of tea and watched the girl sympathetically. Then Stella, in her distraction, pulled a magazine out from her backpack. The feature article was called

"How to be Popular."

"You careless girl!" yelled her Grandmother from behind her, "Why did your parents come over here? Without your discipline, their efforts will amount to nothing!" Chastened, Stella slapped the cover shut and worked out math problems in her notebook.

When the loud creak finally came from the front door, it was past 8:30. Stella had studied math, mostly, for two hours. She had to get an A, which she could if she studied hard. Apba counted on her, and so did Eileen. Without her math achievement, Stella felt that she just might disappear. She would rather have been reading books, pretending that she was living other lives, in other places, away from there, but she knew what her father would ask. She was glad she had finished. As her mother entered, Stella jumped up and squirmed past her Grandmother, running toward the door. Her mother struggled with three bags of groceries. Stella and her Grandmother carried them into the kitchen.

Mrs. Kim's smooth black hair was neatly combed, but flat. She stood in the foyer, putting her coat away. Her flowered polyester dress was wrinkled, and her feet were swollen in their thin white socks, Stella noticed as her mother slipped off her shoes. When she had worked as a nurse, Mrs. Kim dressed better. Stella wished that she could help her parents more at work.

When her mother came into the kitchen and hugged her, Stella felt enveloped in safety again, but the moment was too short. Mrs. Kim pulled away from her daughter and walked upstairs to put away her purse, rubbing her swollen wrist as she went. Stella stood at the bottom of the stairs, watching, and knew that her mother wouldn't go to see the doctor.

Mr. Kim came in soon after, having put the car away in the garage. He walked unseeing past Stella, past the groceries, past the sound of Frankie shrieking, toward his routine shower. He hated the smells of his job and wouldn't do anything before he washed. Stella couldn't understand this, sometimes, and Frankie's shrieking jarred her nerves. She scowled.

When her mother came down the stairs, her eyes widened a little to see her long-haired young daughter with such a sour expression. Resting a hand on her daughter's tight shoulder, they walked together into the kitchen. Stella sat at the table, as expected, her math book open.

The familiar dark circles under her mother's eyes made her look older. She smiled at Stella and carefully set the prepared food on a tray. Stella tipped the cover of her math book closed and pushed it aside. She got up to help. Wordlessly, her mother placed one hand on Stella's arm, and she returned to her seat and her math. There was something here, like kim chee, that was stronger than Stella, that she didn't understand. Father preferred to have mother serve him, so that is what she did first. He also preferred to see his daughter studying, especially math. He was a traditional man, Grandmother said, a strong Korean man. Stella wondered if being strong meant being served by others.

The smell of ammonia distracted Stella from her work. She stood up to see her father, who stopped two steps above her on the stairs. He was tall, for a Korean man, with thick hair, a square jaw and intense dark eyes. His hair had only begun to gray. He didn't smile often. A few drops of water from his wet hair sprinkled Stella's face.

"Have you been a good girl today? How is your math? I hope that you are the best in the class," he said in Korean, though he knew English well enough to have worked here as an engineer. Stella didn't understand why he had quit and opened a dry cleaning business. He seemed ashamed of it, so Stella helped him and kept their business a secret. Before answering his question, Stella looked around for her Grandmother, who might yell at her for telling a lie. Grandmother seemed to be in the laundry room again.

"Neh, Apba," she replied, saying 'yes' respectfully in his native language. He could speak English, but Stella guessed that he didn't like to because he had an accent. He nodded in satisfaction at her answer, then looked toward the kitchen where the sauteeing kim chee stew smelled spicy and warm.

"Then study now," he replied.

Stella's finger twirled the end of her hair into a knot. She hovered outside the dining room for some time, watching her parents eat. She wished she could give her mother a neckrub, or just be near her father's strength for a little while. They didn't invite her to join them. Resignedly, she started walking toward the stairs. On the way, she glanced at the kitchen clock. It was after nine, and Eileen would have left for the mall already. Anxiety tugged at her stomach, as she thought about the birthday party. She walked upstairs.

Chapter 2

Charlie Chan, Part I

Despite the dark, gray sky outside the cleaning store, it was only 10 a.m. Stella shook out her hands as she stood at the counter. On a Saturday at the shop she wrote more than she did during a day at school. Her schoolbooks lay in a pile, unopened, on the counter. There was so much work to do. Her parents would work into the night, doing maintenance and alterations, long after Stella would leave to go home for dinner.

For the last few minutes, there had been no customers dropping off or picking up clothes. She glanced down at the pile of stamped envelopes on the glass-topped counter.

Maybe she would mop up the floor where customers had trudged in slush and mud with heavy wet boots or soiled sneakers. She walked to the closet and pulled out the yellow-handled, gray-roped mop and started to wipe the slush from the flecked linoleum floor. Through the storefront's plate-glass windows, the mini-mall's black-topped parking lot looked like a lumpy gray stew. The long, heavy mop strained her shoulders.

Through the glass, Stella saw plain cars, like her parents', and expensive cars, like Eileen's parents', pull in and out of the lot. She scrutinized the traffic, but the Engleharts' black Volvo wasn't there. She relaxed a little.

After making a last little swirl, Stella hoisted the mop to her waist to carry it to the sink. As she pushed through the hanging plastic bags toward the back of the store, the shadows touched her like little fingers up and down her arms. She shivered.

When she approached the middle of the store, the air pressed against her like a hand; it was heavy, and it was hot. Although fluorescent bulbs buzzed overhead, the clothes piled in the corners suffocated the light so that the store seemed dark. Like a novice swordswoman, Stella bravely stabbed the shadows with the mop, as she hurried toward the clearing.

In the middle of the store lay a refuge for her family. Some light filtered in through the windows, illuminating long steel cones, bottles of liquid, and an iron powered by a long red cord. The air smelled sterile, plastic, chemical. She passed her mother, who was bent over her sewing machine, repairing impossible rips put there by careless people. The fabric always looked seamless when Mrs. Kim finished. Grandmother always said, "Your mother's hands are special; they heal people, they heal clothes, they never stop their work to mend."

Stella now approached her father, who ran the towering machines and wall of controls in the back. These thick knobs and crude equipment were so different from the sterile drafting table and precise calculations he had made as an engineer. Stella had been to his office once, in downtown Chicago, along with her brothers. It had been in a high-rise, and he had worked in a bright, clean room. Like the other men in the office, he wore a suit and tie. Unlike them, he never spoke, responding stiffly to his colleagues' casual friendliness. They seemed to respect him, as far as Stella could tell, and his work looked clean and detailed. It couldn't have been bad. She couldn't understand why he left that job. This store was so dark and clumsy, and the work was so physically hard. She arrived at the utility sink to the left of the machines, and turned on the water to rinse the heavy mop.

This mechanical world, in the farthest, darkest corner of the shop was her father's dominion. Over the churning machines blared the high tinny sound of the Korean radio station. He created his own world back there. Apba heaped clothes into an industrial green-colored machine as big as a firetruck, and a sharp smell like ammonia wafted toward her, despite the fans whirring overhead near the long fluorescent lights. He didn't notice her. She turned off the spigot, wrung out the mop and tucked it under her arm.

The silver bell over the front door rang. The ironing equipment, chemicals, and steam iron cluttered her path. Before she pushed aside the looming wall of plastic bags, it rang again. Stella clenched her teeth and stepped around the equipment.

She burst through the clothes, still holding the mop, and looked around with a sinking heart. She had lost a customer; her parents would be angry. Then she noticed a pile of mail on the counter. The packet of stamped envelopes was gone. With relief, Stella hurriedly shoved the mop into the closet and picked up the mail.

"Apba!" she yelled to her father, "it's the mail!" She walked toward the back again, deliberately sorting the envelopes. Mrs. Kim looked up from her work by the window as Stella walked by, turned off the old iron machine, and folded a pink silk dress.

Mr. Kim wiped the sweat off his forehead before reaching for the stack of mail. Stella smiled, but looked down. The family came together in the middle of the store. Stella opened the small refrigerator and took out a sweating pitcher of barley tea. Stella poured the tea into a chipped ceramic cup as her father sat down heavily on an old folding chair. Stella poured a second cup for her mother. Finally, Stella sat down too.

"Hey!"

All three heads turned toward the front. Stella jumped up.

"Herrow, you! Charlie Chan! Mama-san!" Bing bing bing bing bing, went the bell. "How about some service?" Stella's mother and father looked at each other. Their glances were loaded with meaning that Stella didn't understand.

"Sit down, Sung Ok," said Stella's father in Korean, "I will go to this one." He got out of his chair and pushed back his sleeves.

Stella watched as her mother scrambled to her feet. Striving to outpace her husband, she called, "Just a minute, sir. Be right there!"

Bing bing bing went the bell. Stella got up and followed her parents a few steps toward the front. Mother reached the counter first. "Can I help you?" she asked politely, reaching to examine the clothes on the counter. Stella's father stood off to the side.

"Hey, Charlie Chan! How ya doin'?" The man waved. He had greasy hair and wore his workshirt untucked. "No tickee no shirtee!" Mr. Kim stared, motionlessly. Stella's stomach twisted into a small tight knot. In the meantime, Stella's mother had taken the shirts and walked swiftly away toward the front window and held them up to the light. "Comere, Mr. Chan!" yelled the man, ignoring Mrs. Kim. "Lemme show you this stain. Ancient Chinese secret!"

"What is the stain on this one? Where is it? Could you show me exactly?" asked Mrs. Kim insistently. Stella knew that her mother could see the stain. She was making herself sound stupid. The man finally followed her there to explain, and Mr. Kim unclenched his fists.

"Come with me, Sung Ok." Her father retreated to the back. He sat in his chair and lifted his cup. "Sit down." As he studied Stella's face, her stomach twisted tighter and tighter. She couldn't understand any of this. Her father rarely spoke directly to her, and she feared she had done something wrong. Suddenly, her father stood up and said, "Listen to what your Grandmother says." He walked away toward the hot heavy air in the back of the store. The basement door slammed shut. Feeling confused, Stella watched him go. She looked around helplessly, and settled on putting away the cups.

Around two o'clock, when her mother and father were busy ironing and packaging the laundered shirts, Stella decided to help her parents by sorting clothes. First, she lined up several of the rolling, white-cloth sided carts. Then, she reached into mountain of heavy, soiled clothing and looked at the label on each piece. Finally, she threw each piece into a cart according to its fabric so that her parents could wash more efficiently. The carts filled up quickly; there were different piles for rayon, linen, cotton-blends, polyester, and silk. As she immersed herself in this work, her math and spelling books remained forgotten. When she finished filling the carts, Stella smiled to herself.

When she pushed the first big cart behind the hanging clothes, her parents looked up. Stella's bangs were sweaty and her blue shirt was wrinkled. She looked like her mother did after work. Instead of smiling, her father frowned and turned his back. Her mother put down the iron and walked over to Stella, shaking her head.

"Sung Ok," Mother said, "this is not your work. Go back up front. Study. We do not want to see you back here." Stella's father lowered the iron's pressing arm roughly and it hissed as the hot wet air unwrinkled the cloth. As she walked back to the front of the store, she heard her father raising his voice, as if arguing, although her mother didn't argue back.

When the sun started to fall in the late afternoon, the flow of customers fell off. Stella hadn't studied at all, because the customers needed her full attention, she reasoned. When the store had been empty for a quarter hour, her Grandmother's words echoed in her mind, "It is better to work with your brain than with your back." She wondered if this was what her parents were upset about. In the darkening light, she cracked open her math book.

Close to closing time, as she looked over some spelling words, a woman customer asked Stella about herself. As her mother listened nearby, Stella said that she was in seventh grade, liked math, and on Saturdays, she helped her parents at work.

When the husband came to help her carry out the clothes, the woman said, "She speaks English so well for an Oriental!" Stella sucked in air through her teeth, and willed her face to stay expressionless, but her shoulders rose in anger. Her mother stepped to the front, but Stella squeezed out in a soft, controlled voice, "I was born here." By then, the woman was gone.

Under the buzzing fluorescent lights, Stella was left alone, watching the cars pulling in and out of the lot. She looked up, and in the plate glass windows saw the reflection of a small pretty girl with a frown, standing at a counter, doing problems from a math book.

Chapter 3

The Border of Popularity

The boys stood like a forest in the hallway; Jesse towered, and the others looked young and reedy. His height seemed to attract the attention of the popular girls. They looked at him, one at a time, and giggled. The boys pretended to ignore them, as they swayed on their enormous feet and bobbed and hit one another, as if replaying their championship basketball game. His fair skin, slightly upturned nose and wide, soft smile set off by brown-black eyes and hair, Jesse looked over his shoulder.

"Hi, Stel." He smiled warmly before turning back to his friends.

"Hi," she whispered, eyes darting around until she saw them. Eileen and her friends stood in a tight little circle outside the homeroom door. Eileen was clearly their leader. She was average height, similar to Stella, but bony where Stella was muscular, fair where Stella was dark, and pinched where Stella was rounded. Eileen and her friends all wore pink and purple. Their long hair hung loose. Stella bit her upper lip. Her hair was braided, her clothes a mixture of yellow and green. Thinking of her Grandmother, she took a deep breath and approached them.

Three heads of long hair whipped around as the girls turned their heads away, forming a shield.

"Here comes Stella," whispered one, "look at that — yellow and green, just like Eileen told her to wear!" One voice dug into her spine like a knife. Another chimed in, saying "April Fool's!" Stella clutched her books to her chest and abandoned her hopes. She escaped the hallway and fled into the classroom.

The classroom's harsh fluorescent light stung Stella's eyes. Behind her in the hallway, their teacher spoke with one of the parents. Stella halted. The parent's voice sounded familiar. When the popular girls filed into the classroom, toward their seats by the door where they watched and judged, Stella felt pushed forward into the middle of the room.

The artificial light was less intense by the windows. Rachel sat alone by the classroom's outside wall, tall and striking, her auburn hair masking her face as she stared down at her books. Her gold-flecked Indian scarf set off the blue in her cabled sweater, and her strong, balanced features were untouched by efforts at makeup. Behind Rachel was a wall of glass, a window to the changing, turbulent weather. A moody blue had crept into the sky, hinting of darkness, but still holding the promise of light.

Stella's heavy backpack pulled at her arm. She sat close to Rachel, but not too close. In a circle by the door the popular girls sat together, surrounding Eileen like petals on a flower. Not knowing what else to do, Stella pretended to study math.

"And after the spelling bee and my party," said Eileen, "we'll try out for cheerleading together." Eileen's pointed chin bobbed rapidly as she talked, and her little freckled nose pulled to a point as she sniffed out compliments or advantage. The girls nodded their heads in agreement, and Amanda glanced out the door before leaning to whisper something in Eileen's ear. The two girls giggled wildly, and Eileen craned her neck to see Jesse outside the door. The bell rang.

As the boys tumbled into the classroom, Eileen watched Jesse closely. When Jesse and his best friend, Marcus, hit each other, the popular girls giggled. Stella didn't notice Jesse bumping her desk as he passed. She only thought of how far she was from Eileen these days. Rachel looked over at Stella and smiled, but Stella felt as if she couldn't afford to smile back. If Stella lived on the border of popularity, then Rachel inhabited a different universe.

"Well, of course I'll notify the Booster paper and the Chicago Tribune," came the clipped, high voice from the hallway. "The spelling bee is, after all, one of our school's proudest traditions,

and we need to communicate our students' achievements."
Mrs. Murphy, who stood in view just outside the door, smiled
primly with her bright-red lips at the person speaking.

It was Eileen's mother, Mrs. Englehart. Eileen beamed. Her
mother didn't work outside the home, so she visited school
often. She was the P.T.A. president and a school board member.
More importantly, she had won their school's spelling bee as a
student, and her family had lived in this town for 50 years.

"Mrs. Murphy gives too much homework. She should be
nicer," said Amanda, "and she's too bossy. She bosses your
mom around, Eileen."

"Yeah," agreed Heather.

"Well, I think she's the nicest teacher I've ever met," said
Eileen.

"Oh, I didn't mean that I didn't like, like her," Amanda said,
hurriedly, "I just mean that I don't like her giving so much
work."

"I think she's great," said Eileen.

"I think so, too," said Heather, Eileen's other friend. Eileen
smiled at Heather and excluded Amanda. Amanda said, "I
really like her, too. I really, really like her." The girls crowded
together again. On Stella's other side, Rachel put her finger in
her mouth, pretending to gag.

"Yes," came Mrs. Murphy's voice from the hallway, swinging
her hand up to smooth her lacquered hair, "the prevailing

student should be widely recognized, I agree."

"Wouldn't that be a joke if your princess lost," muttered Rachel from her seat by the windows. It was like the voice of a ghost, or a conscience. You never even saw Rachel's lips move. "All she cares about is cheerleading," Rachel continued. "She's not tough enough to compete academically." Her shocking green-blue eyes glinted intensely, but she smiled at Stella. Stella's soft eyes smiled back, although sometimes she couldn't understand what Rachel meant.

The discussion in the hallway continued. "I want you to know that I protested this ludicrous multicultural curriculum requirement, but it was pointless. Political correctness has carried the day again," said Mrs. Englehart, who had stepped in front of the door. Eileen's mother was tall and angular, with faded blond hair pulled sharply into a bun. She wore a tweed suit in a pale tan color, and looked like a long, beige stick. She towered over Mrs. Murphy. Rachel turned her eyes toward the women talking.

"Yes, well, we will always be riding the latest fad in education. Why, I remember in the 1970s. . . "

Stella looked around the classroom. In the back of the room, Marcus studied, and Jesse slept with his eyes open again. He was definitely unusual, Stella thought. If he weren't so cute, Eileen would never like him. He frustrated Stella, because he got better grades than she did without studying. She was expected to be the best in math, but often he was. A small shock of static electricity sparked her hand, and she jerked it back in shock. The charged air caught her attention. It was time to study.

One problem confounded her. When she leaned over to ask for Rachel's help, she heard a "tch" sound shot at her like a bullet. Stella looked up to see Eileen's bony shoulder jerking in her direction. "Well, some people will do anything to keep their grades above everyone else's," Eileen announced, raising her chin in the air, "they don't mind showing off, bringing attention to themselves." Stella dropped her hand on her book and stared at Eileen, her mouth open in disbelief.

"Some people think they're superior," Eileen said, glaring directly at Stella. Eileen's small light eyes glinted meanly in the fluorescent light. For a moment, everything stood still, and Stella felt all the heads in the classroom turning to stare at her. This attention fatigued her, tortured her. She wanted to melt into the floor. When she looked around the classroom, she saw everyone staring at her except for Jesse, of course.

Stella remembered that she had forgotten to call Eileen Friday. Then last night, she had forgotten to call her again to help her get ready for today's math test. Stella dropped her head onto her hand, and wondered how she could have been so stupid. At the same time, however, she felt a singing in her heart that made no sense.

"That girl is a creep," Rachel's voice spoke again, "and those girls are pathetic little slaves." Stella didn't know what to think or where to look. Rachel just didn't understand how things were.

"Thank you so much for your time, Mrs. Murphy," said Mrs. Englehart from the hallway. "The children are waiting, au revoir!"

The heavy wooden door slammed shut. Mrs. Murphy swept into the class, her curled brown-gray hair looking stiff and smelling like a seaful of chemicals.

"Hello to the world," mocked Rachel, only halfway under her breath. "She thinks her class is the universe. She thinks she's the Almighty God." Stella closed her mouth and looked straight ahead. If she sat quietly, then maybe everyone would leave her alone.

"Bonjour tout le monde, my little world!" said the teacher, sailing past the front row to her desk.

"Et bonjour a vous, Madame," responded Eileen, sitting up straight and folding together her short bony hands. Eileen's friends raised their heads and sat up, too, like flowers following the sun. A chortling sound came from the the boys in the back of the room. Mrs. Murphy opened her briefcase and pulled out a red pen. Her smile vanished. "Proceed to study."

"Rachel. . . " Stella whispered, leaning toward her friend's desk. Outside the windows, big drops of rain fell slowly. Rachel pulled back her thick hair and smiled warmly. "Can you explain this?" As Rachel leaned over to look, Mrs. Murphy interrupted.

"Is this a social hour, Miss Weintraub?"

Rachel raised her reddish, arched eyebrow and shrugged. Stella clenched her fist and glared at the teacher, who smiled in return. "What am I, invisible?" grumbled Stella. "It was my fault." In the meantime, Eileen jumped up and approached the teacher's desk. Stella looked down at her textbook.

"What a fakey little brown-noser," muttered Rachel. Eileen stood at the desk, which had pinned upon it a photo of last year's spelling bee champions. Eileen was the runner-up. From across the room, the other popular girls looked at Stella and pointed. When Eileen noticed, and laughed, too, Stella's heart sank. She was outside again, and there was only one way to change that.

She ripped a piece of paper out of her spiral notebook. Her stomach flipped crazily, and she clutched it with one hand. On the paper, she wrote: "I'm sorry about forgetting to call you. I'll help you with math over lunch." She folded the paper in to a little packet, addressed it to Eileen and wrote "PRIVATE" in big square letters across the back. The tearing sound of the bell hit her at the same time as the pain ripped through her abdomen. It consumed her, until a noise from the back of the room distracted her attention.

Jesse had coughed when he woke up. He sat up now, a long-sleeved t-shirt covering his broad shoulders, running one long, slim finger down each page of the math book. Stella shook her head. He had told Rachel that he hadn't studied for today's test. Anger welled up in her. It seemed so unfair. When Eileen and her friends arose to leave together, Stella's whole heart followed their every movement. With a short glance at Rachel, Stella clutched the folded paper in her palm. As she rushed toward the doorway, Mrs. Murphy appeared at Stella's side.

"Well, my dear, I see that you're not entering the spelling bee this year." Stella looked at the teacher mutely, her pride daring her to do the opposite. Nevertheless, her eyebrows shot up hopefully when Eileen slipped between them and said brightly,

"Stella's going to coach me this year, Mrs. Murphy. Aren't you, Stella?" Stella fingered her folded note and noticed the popular girls watching her from outside the door. "I really want to be in that picture again this year, Mrs. Murphy," Eileen concluded. Eileen quickly left Stella and rejoined them.

"Well . . . well," said the teacher, laying her fleshy hand on Stella's shoulder, "that's most appropriate. Are you still practicing, my dear?" she asked, the thick powder flaking off her skin, "You people have such a lovely musical tradition." Her red lips cracked into a smile. Stella's heart leaped in anger. She didn't even play the piano.

She turned her back and walked down the locker-lined hallway toward her social studies class. In the flow of rushing students, Stella moved easily down the hall while her mind stretched backward. She tried to remember the last time that she had seen that smile. Then it came to her; it had been last fall when she and her parents had seen Mrs. Murphy. . .

❦

The air had been crisp and cold, not heavy and soft like it was today. It had been in September, right after the school's open house. Her mother's car had been in the shop, so both her parents had met her at school for the soccer team meeting. She wasn't allowed to go to the store during the week.

On the way down the hall, her father had told her that he was interested in helping with the team. When Stella had explained to him that the coach was a woman, and that practices were held every afternoon, they both looked concerned. Stella realized that they couldn't afford her to be absent from home every afternoon, and she knew that she wouldn't go out for the team. None of this was stated, however, and they continued walking toward Mrs. Factor's room. Then Eileen had run out of their homeroom.

"Stella!" she had said, pulling on her coat. "You didn't tell me that you were trying out for the talent show!"

"I'm not," Stella replied softly, "I'm trying out for . . ." Mrs. Murphy interrupted them.

"Miss Kim! And these must be your parents. How do you do," she had said, "I expect that your daughter will perform a musical piece for our show?" Her red plastic smile shone like neon.

"I don't play any instrument," Stella said stubbornly but softly, "I was here for soccer." Her mother watched her closely. They didn't like it when she challenged adults.

"Yes, well, our meeting will begin in ten minutes," said Mrs. Murphy, as if Stella hadn't spoken, "we're waiting for some of those children from the soccer tryout to find their way over here."

Mr. Kim stood stoically behind his daughter. "Your parents would be so proud to have you participate in the talent show," Mrs. Murphy said, pointing at Stella's parents. Stella squirmed. It was considered extremely rude to point at people in Korean culture. In addition, Mrs. Murphy had met her mother at last month's open house. Her father was stiff and silent, looking away. He understood everything but wouldn't speak up, because of his pride. Stella felt angry that he wouldn't speak English. To Stella's relief, Mrs. Kim stepped in.

"We are pleased to see you," she said in her most careful English, "Stella has told us . . ."

"Oh, I am so pleased to meet you, too," said Mrs. Murphy. "Stella is such a dear girl. So obedient. Well," she said, laying her hand on Mrs. Kim's arm, "I must finish preparing for this meeting. So nice to have met you," she winked at Mr. Kim and turned around toward Eileen. Mr. Kim's jerk backward was almost imperceptible. It was a few seconds before Stella noticed her mother pulling gently at her arm. Stella's feet felt cemented to the floor. She wondered what it would take for people to notice them, to take her family seriously.

If she could have explained to her parents that she understood about soccer, that she didn't have to join the team, she would have just left the school then and there. Such a discussion was impossible for reasons that she could only sense, but never explain.

Her face burned as she guided her parents through this unfamiliar world. Anger shot through her heart, looking for a target. If only her parents could act like everyone else, then maybe Mrs. Murphy wouldn't treat her like this, she thought, glancing at her handsome proud father and her sensitive, kind mother. Her mind and heart whirled in confusion, not knowing what to feel or think.

Stella walked down the hallway, thinking about Mrs. Murphy's plastic smile — the same smile from last fall when she expected Stella to play the piano just because she was Korean.

❦

She shook her head back into Monday and realized that, while she was thinking, she had walked all the way to Ms. Queen's class. She felt some anger that her parents couldn't speak English, even though they had lived in this country for thirteen years already. She felt jealous of Eileen for having such powerful, perfect parents. At the same time, Stella felt angry at Eileen's attitude toward her. Popularity was a complicated problem, one that she didn't want to think about anymore that day. She felt relieved to be going to Ms. Queen's class, where she would be challenged intellectually but treated with respect. Near the door to Ms. Queen's class, Eileen stood with her circle of friends.

"Lice . . . " Stella thought she overheard from the group of popular girls. She looked up, said hello, and made herself hand her note to Eileen before the flowing crowd pushed her into the room.

Chapter 4

Garlic and Gyros

At lunch it continued to rain. As Stella stepped into the vast, linoleum-tiled cafeteria, the sickly-spicy smell of Sloppy Joes covered her nose like a dirty washcloth.

She passed closely by Ms. Queen, who monitored the lunchroom. Her turquoise earrings sparkled. She lay a hand on Stella's shoulder and said, "Smile, Stella! Life isn't so serious! Maybe Wednesday's field trip will brighten your week!" The teacher's sky-blue eyes sparkled like the turquoise. Stella felt a fresh breeze in her spirit. There was something . . . respectful and independent about Ms. Queen.

From across the room, Eileen waved Stella to the homeroom table. At first, she felt horrified, then hopeful. She looked all around before responding. Eileen wasn't waving at anyone else. Stella smiled tentatively and stepped toward the popular group.

"Stella, hi!" Eileen beamed at her and slid over to offer Stella a seat. "Isn't lunch gross today?" Her pert, up-turned nose wrinkled as she smiled. "I'm not eating either." Stella struggled to figure out Eileen's meaning. Had she gotten the note? It was hard for her to tell what was real. The day's rain had crowded out the sun, and Eileen's face shone weirdly under the lights.

"The weather's gross today, too." Eileen shrugged her pointed shoulders, "Let's sit together in homeroom for recess, okay?"

Stella nodded gratefully at her thin blonde friend and sat down. Rachel passed by their table on her way to the food line, seeming not to notice Stella or Eileen.

Eileen whispered, "Can you believe how she looks? Her hair is so scraggly and long!" Eileen's teeth flashed and Stella grimaced, half-hoping that Eileen would think it was a smile.

"I think she's so . . . different, don't you think?" Eileen continued. "She knows she'll never fit in anyway, so she doesn't even try . . . Why, did you know that her mother . . ."

The flash of Rachel's orange lunch tray caught Stella's eye, and she abruptly turned away. Rachel sat down and frowned over her chocolate milk and carrots. Stella flushed.

"Hi, Rachel! We were just saying how nice you look . . ." she smirked, knowingly. "Weren't we, Stella?" She displayed another big smile and touched Stella on the arm, as if they shared a secret. Stella pulled her arm away, just a little.

"Your lunch looks great," Eileen continued. "Stella and I can't stand to eat anything at all, though. We feel just the same about it." Stella felt relieved and looked over at the food line. She was always hungry at lunchtime. There was a bowl of oranges next to the cash register. . . She raised herself up from the table. Maybe Rachel and Eileen would get along if they were alone for a while, she thought hopefully.

"Stella, what would you pick if you could eat anything in the world you wanted right now?" Eileen asked her. She sat back down.

"Pizza," she said, "but Chicago style, not the little squares they serve us here for lunch." She looked from Eileen to Rachel, hoping that they could all agree on something.

"I love stir-fry," said Eileen to Stella. Rachel concentrated on putting the carrot sticks in a row.

"I don't," said Stella, a little too loudly.

"Stella, you do too like stir-fry. Don't tell me you never eat it. What are you, Greek?" Eileen shook with laughter.

"Stella never eats stir-fries." Rachel spoke softly, without looking up. "She doesn't like them. That's Chinese style, anyway. She doesn't like sushi, either. That's Japanese style." Rachel raised her head and looked at Stella. "But," she said, "Stella loves gyros. Any size, flavor, or at any time of day. Gyros, gyros, gyros. That's all she ever eats." Stella smiled at her friend, who finally eyed Eileen. "All you eat is hot dogs and pizza, I suppose? Or does your mom — I mean, your maid — cook gourmet dinners every night?"

Eileen looked wildly around the room for her friends, but they weren't there. She smoothed her hair back rapidly two or three times. Rachel's gaze did not flinch. Eileen looked ready to cry when she sputtered, "Well, I know that's not true. At Stella's house . . . I've been to Stella's house, you know. You haven't, have you Rachel?" Eileen glared at Rachel and continued, ". . . she doesn't eat gyros there. Don't be idiotic, Rachel," she said, flipping back her hair from her eyes which now gleamed with anger, "It's a house full of Oriental foods. I don't know which KIND, specifically. I mean, really. Who cares which KIND. Oriental food is all you can smell. In fact, the whole house smells of GARLIC. Nothing but garlic!" Eileen laughed. "Isn't that right, Stella?" Eileen turned to her. "Garlic."

Stella bit her upper lip and looked down at the table for a moment. She felt that time wasn't passing — that this day was just frozen and would never end. When she finally did look up, she caught Rachel watching her with concern. Stella felt lucky when the bell rang and everyone else got up from the table and left. She and Eileen were alone.

"Stella," Eileen said after pausing for a moment, "I haven't been to your house for . . ." Eileen looked up toward the ceiling and thought, "for over a year?" Her behavior seemed different to Stella, softer. Memories of their years of friendship rushed back to Stella, and she felt full of everything she needed to tell Eileen. She had just opened her mouth when the second bell rang.

Eileen hooked their arms together. Stella smiled. Eileen pulled Stella and said, "Come on. If we don't hurry, Murphy will mark us late for recess. You still have to help me with math." Stella stared wonderingly, until Eileen continued, "Math, you know, math! As in, the test today? Or have you forgotten, Miss Yellow Girl?" Stella's deep brown eyes shone with unshed tears. At least she hadn't said anything. Allowing Eileen to pull her along, they passed Rachel in the hallway on their way inside. Rachel just watched.

You're So Lucky

Stella's thick dark hair felt like a wet blanket. The cold spring rain flattened it against her back as she trudged home from school. As she left school, she carefully wrapped her scarf over her suede and denim bookbag. Her hat never even came out of her pocket. No one wore hats, let alone in early April. She shivered.

Her plaid socks and leather shoes were so soaked that she didn't even bother to step around puddles. She occasionally wiped the water off her face which had paled to the color of ivory, in stark contrast to her wet dark hair and navy blue coat. "Perfect ending to a perfect day," she muttered to herself as a car sped by, splashing water on her legs. She rubbed her eyes.

"I just want to go home, watch T.V. and be left alone. With any luck, those idiots will be somewhere else." She turned right into her driveway and knew, even before she pushed open the heavy white door, that the boys were home.

The T.V. blared from downstairs. The kitchen light was off. Stella smelled the faint scent of smoke and knew that Grandmother was in the laundry room again. She threw her wet bookbag against the back of the couch and walked downstairs. She shoved Frankie off the good chair and settled down to watch reruns of "The Brady Bunch." Grandmother walked past them with a basketful of laundry.

"Sung Ok!" she called from the living room. "Go take some snacks to your brothers. I am busy. They are growing boys and need their sister's support. Do I have to tell you everything?" Stella glared at Albert and Frankie before she spoke.

"Do I have to do everything? Are your arms broken? Is my job in life to take care of everyone else?"

"What's wrong, Stel?" asked Albert.

"I hate this," cried Stella, sitting up straight in her comfortable chair, "like you're more important than me. Like you don't know where the food is. Why can't I be left alone? Why does she always pick on me? She must hate me! She makes me act Korean all the time, so that everybody thinks I'm weird. I hate her! Why did they have to open that stupid store and ruin my life?" She threw the remote control across the room at Frankie, who caught it. She stomped up the stairs toward the kitchen.

From the cabinet, Stella pulled out two old plastic cups.

"They're just creepy little animals, anyway," she said to herself. "They'll break anything good." One cup bounced onto the floor after she slammed it on the tray. As she reached to pick it up, she heard a crash.

"Aaaaaahhhhh!" yelled Frankie. Stella shook her head and pulled open the freezer door, but Grandmother dropped an undershirt and hurried downstairs. In the rush, her glasses fell off. Stella walked over to pick them up. She would take them downstairs and see what Grandmother was up to in the laundry room.

The phone rang. Carrying Grandmother's glasses, Stella walked over to the phone but, before she could answer it, the doorbell chimed. Stella stood two steps from the phone, five steps from the front door, clutching Grandmother's glasses and the plastic cup.

Stella felt rooted to one spot as the doorbell chimed and the harsh ring sounded. "Move, you idiot!" she told herself, but she didn't budge. Everything pushed in on her at once.

"Sung Ok! Sung Ok! Get down here and take care of your brothers! Where is your mind?" Thunder crashed outside. Then the doorbell chimed again, twice, insistently. Whoever was out there must be getting soaked, she thought. She opened the door.

Rachel's face was nearly hidden in a deep hood. Her black backpack absorbed the rain. She shivered in the cold but smiled.

"Rachel?"

"Hi, Stella. I hope it's okay to stop by. I . . ."

Stella stared as the phone rang and Frankie screamed. Lightning exploded in the distance; Rachel jumped as the thunder boomed.

"Sung Ok! Get down here now!"

"I guess it's a bad time. It's okay," said Rachel, her smile fading and her blue-green eyes looking closely at Stella, who stood clutching glasses and a plastic cup, staring at her. Rachel hoisted her backpack further up on her shoulders. "I'll just go," she said. "See you tomorrow." Rachel turned around to leave.

A gust of cold wind hit Stella in the face as it blew through the open door. The telephone's ringing stopped, and Stella's shoulders relaxed. "Rachel!" she yelled eagerly to her friend's back. "I'm sorry! Come in!"

Stella stood back and opened the door wider as Rachel walked in, dripping wet. As she took off her backpack and coat, Rachel looked toward the sound of screaming in the basement. "Is everything okay?"

"I'll be right back," Stella said. As she rushed down the stairs, the hot, searing smell of burning kim chee floated past. She stopped, shrugged, and asked Rachel, "Do you want a drink?" She took two cans of soda pop out of the refrigerator.

Rachel lugged her backpack into the kitchen and the two

girls sat at the kitchen table. Stella was distracted by the noise from the stairs, the smell of smoking kim chee, and the sight of laundry piled high.

"Well," said Rachel, unzipping her wet bag, "I just wanted to see if you wanted to talk about the spelling bee." The phone rang again.

Stella left the room and picked up the phone. It was Eileen.

"Um, hi," she said, turning her back to the kitchen.

"No, I haven't studied yet," she said timidly, glancing at Rachel's back in the kitchen.

"No, why don't you do it yours–," She stood up straight.

"No, I can't go out Saturdays . . ." She twisted the cord in her hand, "just because. I'm busy. Okay?"

"Bye," she said, but Eileen had already hung up. Stella stood still for a moment before returning to the kitchen.

When Stella returned to the table, Rachel got right down to business. "I think you could win the spelling bee," she said, "I don't have time this year, because of my bat mitzvah, but I thought you could use a coach." Rachel smiled.

"Eileen thinks she can win," Rachel continued. "I heard her say in the hall today you can't spell. She said that she's just asking you to coach to be nice."

Stella looked sharply up at Rachel. A scene from that morning flashed into her mind like the lightning outside. When Stella had passed Eileen and "the groupies" on her way into social studies class, Eileen had said that Orientals like Stella couldn't even pronounce English, let alone spell it.

"I want some flied lice, prease," was what Eileen had said, and they had all laughed, with mean, closed lips.

Even worse, when Stella walked past them, the girls all looked at her and smiled. "Hi, Stella, how are you?" smiled Eileen, and Heather and Amanda had just snorted with laughter and looked away. Stella had pushed the thought away at the time, but now she felt something like hatred. She looked at her friend, expectantly.

Rachel pulled the dark blue spelling booklet out of her packpack. The girls leaned together over the round white table and looked at the list of beginning words. "Tell me if you know how to spell these," said Rachel, taking out a pencil. "If you do, we'll go straight to the intermediate list." Stella nodded.

"Sung Ok," the voice broke into the air from the top of the stairs. Stella jumped. Grandmother walked in the doorway, pulling a confused-looking Frankie by the ear. He had a bandage on his forehead, which he rubbed carefully.

Stella mouthed the words, "You idiot."

"You never teach your brothers!" Grandmother yelled in Korean. "The soccer ball was in the basement again! They're stupid, just boys. So they play! Why not? Grandmother always repairs your carelessness!" Frankie, still holding his head, leaned away from her loud, high-pitched voice.

As she dragged Frankie into the kitchen, Grandmother noticed Rachel, who sat out of sight in the corner. Grandmother stopped short and smiled at Rachel.

"You're in the kitchen! Drinking from cans? You have given her no food?" She pushed away Frankie, who stared at Rachel with wide eyes and crinkled his nose in a smile.

"Give food to your guests!" Grandmother went to pick up the laundry. Stella took two glasses from the cabinet. When the old woman began peeling an apple, they left for the living room. Grandmother pushed the full tray at Stella.

"Now sit with your friend. Care for your brothers later. Don't have bad manners!" Grandmother smoothed Stella's wild hair, and then slapped Stella gently on the shoulder. Stella was so surprised at her Grandmother's behavior that she didn't hear Rachel talking at first.

" . . . died a year ago. She was just like your Grandmother. Even though she always yelled at me in Yiddish, I miss her. She didn't live with us, though. You're lucky."

In the kitchen, Stella heard her Grandmother scraping the burned kim chee into the garbage. She realized that ever since her parents opened their business, she has come to expect Grandmother to take care of everything. And she did. The kitchen was silent. Even though they fought, Stella was never by herself at home, and they always ate well. Stella listened carefully until she heard her Grandmother working again.

The girls settled into the couch. Rachel quizzed Stella, who spelled nearly every word perfectly. Rachel's hazel eyes gleamed with satisfaction, and Stella's brown eyes sparkled with surprise. "I thought all I could do was math," she said to Rachel, who shook her head.

"It's good to surprise people, especially if they stereotype you," Rachel responded. As time passed, Stella continued to do well. When they finished the beginning section, they stopped to have a snack.

Rachel craned her neck to look over Stella's shoulder. Albert and Frankie's heads poked up from the stairs. "They're cute. Are they your little brothers?" It was all they needed. Albert and Frankie hurled themselves upstairs as if they had been shot from a gun.

They slapped one another and grabbed fistfuls of neon orange cheese curls. Grandmother appeared out of nowhere and said, "Leave your sister alone. She works seriously now. You emulate her, not play with her." With a last look at Rachel, Albert and Frankie retreated to the rec room. Once the boys went downstairs, Grandmother returned to the kitchen. It was nearly dinner time. Grandmother had stood up for Stella; she sat up taller.

"What about the intermediate words?" she asked Rachel, who was zipping up her backpack to go.

"I could come over on Sunday to help you study . . ."

"No, I can't. Sunday's the only day we all spend together. We go to Korean church in Chicago and usually never get home before five o'clock, because I go to Youth Group. And then, when we come home, I have to help with dinner. . ."

"What about Saturday? I don't have to spend that long at the synagogue. I could be over here by . . ."

The phone's ringing broke in on them. Stella looked at Rachel for a moment, and then got up to answer it. Her stomach twisted, not so much because of the lie she was about to tell Rachel, but because she knew who it would be.

"Um, hi," she said to Eileen.

"Um," Stella raised her eyebrows, "yes, you looked great today," she said softly. She glanced at Rachel, who marked the intermediate word list with a short yellow pencil. Her head was cocked at a strange angle.

"Oh, you're going to the mall together to get stuff for your birthday party?" Stella twisted her now-dry hair around her finger. She looked down at her awkward clothes. Her feelings confused her. She hated going to the mall, even though it was what everybody did. Yet the party would be in a few weeks, and Eileen hadn't invited Stella yet. The other popular girls had been invited. ". . at eight-thirty? But that's when my par. . . Okay. Yes, yes. I'll help you."

"No," she sighed, just peeking at Rachel and then turning her back slightly, "not. . . myself. Coach . . . Of. . ."

"Goodbye," she looked at the phone which had gone dead. Stella looked with soft eyes toward her Grandmother for reassurance, but Grandmother stood not looking at her, busy at the stove. The old lady shook her head and furrowed her brow, deep in thought.

Rachel's pencil stopped moving. Blushing, Stella looked down and shrugged. A thought crowded into her mind like a cartoon balloon over a character's head: nothing is fair in seventh grade.

A feeling like dozens of steel toothpicks dug into her stomach. She frowned and looked at her Grandmother and Rachel, who had both begun working again. She returned to the couch and said, "It was just . . . Jesse. He . . . wanted help with math." Rachel looked at her carefully and then looked away. Everyone knew that Jesse never studied.

❧

That night, at 11:30, Rachel was long gone; Eileen hadn't been home when Stella called. At the time, she had felt relieved, but now she was just uncomfortable. She sat on the floor in her room leaning over the small, wooden table, dreaming of being popular. She would be best friends again with Eileen, and they would dress the same and go places together. They would go out to eat — no, to Stella's house — no, to Eileen's house, she guessed, to study. No, they would play. No, they would talk about boys. Stella struggled to think of play. No, they would talk about boys. Stella struggled to think of what they would do together now. Maybe she would have to do things by herself, instead. Her aching neck pulled her attention back to her papers.

She finished her math and was going over the spelling manual. "Okay," she said to herself, rolling her sore neck, "I can do this."

The door opened. Grandmother held a wooden tray with cold barley tea, slices of pear-apple, and chocolate crackers. Stella gratefully pushed away her work. When she saw the spelling manual, Grandmother smiled.

"Don't quit," Grandmother said, pushing the papers back at Stella. "Don't quit." Grandmother laid out the glass and snack plate around Stella's pencils and books and patted the girl on the back. "You work for yourself, for pride, for parents and brothers. Be tough. Smart no good if don't work. Don't quit." Stella, after finding the twinkle of love in her Grandmother's eyes that she had been looking for earlier, released a long breath. She drank some cold tea and picked up her booklet. She barely heard the door slide closed over the deep white carpet.

Chapter 6

Pioneers

The famous Chicago wind swirled around Lincoln Park, flinging empty paper cups and downtown dreams out to the lake. The previous Monday's wet and cold gave way to Wednesday's animation. As the buses pulled in front of the Chicago Historical Society, the sharply-attired young professionals hailed cabs and glanced at their watches. When the buses pulled to a stop with a creak, dozens of children poured out, indistinguishable to adults, but denizens of completely different worlds to the children.

Stella waited in the middle of the bus for the children all around her to empty out. She didn't push; she didn't lead. The popular girls sat together in the front today, the unpopular kids in the back. She felt trapped in the middle, not in the group, and not out of it. The seats around Eileen were taken, and none of those girls would let Stella in.

So she waited, with the other indeterminate children, for the leaders to file out and the teachers to make the way. Mrs. Murphy swirled with excitement. Rachel said, "Look, she's all aglow." Mrs. Murphy came along with the social studies teacher to chaperone the trip. As the students stepped down from the bus, Ms. Queen pulled Stella aside and said, "Pay careful attention to what you see inside."

Stella's eyes were riveted on a woman across the street. In her late 20's, this woman had straw-colored straight hair, an elegant long blue sweater over a perfectly pleated skirt. Her square leather purse hung from a gold chain on her shoulder, and with perfect concentration and confidence, she hailed a cab and glanced at her watch.

Stella glanced at Eileen in her expensive clothes, straight blonde hair, and turned-up nose. The young businesswoman climbed into a cab. Eileen noticed the young woman, who looked remarkably like her, and her friends nudged one another in confirmation of their leader's greatness. After flipping back her hair, Eileen pointed proprietarily to the woman, and then covered her mouth and laughed. Rachel rolled her eyes. Stella noticed with a sinking heart that the cabbie was Asian.

Suddenly, the woman was gone and the wind was sweeping the dozens of students into the pink brick and green glass building in the park. The fresh, sticky smell of the lake flew about their heads with the wind in the naked trees.

Eileen and her friends, along with Mrs. Murphy, led the procession of students. Even though their school arrived second or third, Mrs. Murphy had them going first into the entrance. With the push of students and confusion in the entrance, Stella sought to surge ahead to pick up with Eileen. Rachel, unaware of having been abandoned, fell behind, biting her thumb, looking around the entrance with big eyes. Jesse, who always sat in the last seat on the bus ignoring everybody, hung behind everyone else, and Ms. Queen had to call him back to the group as he opened up the wrong door.

As they entered the pioneer exhibit, Eileen and her followers gasped. A towering canvas seemed to fill the entire room, until they entered and could see that it was an authentic 1811 Conestoga wagon. "This is how my family came here from Baltimore!" cried Eileen, clutching the hands of Amanda and Heather. "Our family has been here for 200 years!" Mrs. Murphy smiled and patted Eileen on the back. After a few moments, Eileen coolly flipped back her chin-length, perfect hair and showed once again that nothing impressed her.

"We came here to learn about the American heritage," Mrs. Murphy said, with that plastic smile.

Once inside the room, where the wagon took up about one half of the exhibit, Stella no longer felt as overwhelmed. It was huge, no doubt. The bowed bottom and the other wood was painted a robin's-egg blue. The wheels were simply black-wooden spoked circles, and a simple white canvas covered the top. There were no seats. Just then, an elderly man in white shirtsleeves and a kind of apron walked into the exhibit.

"In the early 19th century, this was the only way to travel," the man began, smiling at his audience. "Do you notice that there aren't any seats? The families migrating westward to Illinois had to walk the entire distance, covering an average of ten miles per day. Who can tell me why the bottom is curved?"

"So it can float while crossing rivers, like the Ohio, for example," said Rachel, without looking up. How did Rachel know that? Stella wondered.

"Right," said the gentleman. "Which animals pulled the . . ."

"Oh, that's easy!" cut in Eileen, pushing forward through the crowd with her bony shoulders. "Horses! Of course!" she smiled.

"No," the old man said, gently, "they needed a sturdier animal for this kind of burden."

"Oxen," said Jesse, from the back.

"I don't know who said that, but it was correct," said the man, "and have you ever heard of a horse's tail?"

"Of course!" said Eileen, rather assertively. "What a dumb question! It's the tail on a horse!" she said, huffing in disgust and crossing her arms.

"A horse's tail," continued the man without looking at Eileen, "was horsehair attached to a stick which the children of the family would use to chase the flies and hornets off the oxen as they walked so that the beasts wouldn't get irritable and run or upset the wagon. Not a pleasant job," he continued, "in hot humid summer in heavy clothes walking across the prairie."

"I'm sure that my family didn't walk the entire way," said Eileen. "My Grandmother, she told me that my family had horses. This man is just wrong. My family was rich. He's just wrong." Heather nodded in agreement.

"Not only was the walk long and hot, but there often was no trail on the way, and the pioneers would have to wade through streams and rivers at the low points through fast running water. It probably felt good to them, however, considering how hot and sweaty they must have been. Now," he said, looking around at the group, "who besides this young lady had parents who immigrated to the United States?"

It seemed like a trick question. Everyone had, of course. They all looked at one another and some slowly, sheepishly, raised their hands. Stella felt reluctant, but raised hers after everyone else had, too. The old man pointed at Mrs. Murphy. "Where are your folks from, Miss?"

Mrs. Murphy smiled girlishly. "My ancestors are from Ireland and Germany," she said. "They arrived at the end of the last century, on boats. My Grandmother was born on a boat in the Atlantic."

Then the old man looked at Amanda and asked, "And yours, young lady?"

"My family is English," she replied, "I think they came in the 1920s. No, the '50s. I don't know. A war was just over, or something like that." Stella was surprised to see Ms. Queen rolling her eyes.

Then he asked Rachel. "My family came in a ship to New York City from Germany in the 1920s," she responded. Then looking at Ms. Queen with a smile, Rachel added, "Good timing."

Ms. Queen then turned to the exhibit of a printing press across the room and said, "Rachel, weren't your grandparents publishers?" Rachel nodded.

"But I suppose the equipment was more modern than that old set-up," the tour guide said. "Anyone else? How about you, young man?" he asked Jesse.

Jesse responded, "My family came over on the Mayflower, in fact, and lived in Boston for 200 years. They rode the train to Chicago, because they were in the railroad business." Eileen swung her head around and glared at Jesse. Someone else had better ancestors than she did. Then, before Stella could hide, the old man had pointed and asked the same question.

"My family . . . flew here. . . I mean, to Los Angeles."

"From where?" It seemed like everyone was staring at her.

"From . . . from Korea." She turned her back, hoping to

blend into the crowd.

"When?" she heard the old man say. "Miss, when did your family fly here from Korea?" Stella slowly turned back to face the group.

"In. . . 1980," she said softly.

"What? We couldn't hear you," he said with a smile.

"In 1980!" she practically shouted, wishing at the same time that she could melt into the floor.

"Were you even born here?" asked Eileen shrilly. Dozens of faces turned around to look at Stella. "Are you a foreigner?"

"I was born here," said Stella.

Rachel slid up behind her, and whispered, "and so what if you weren't?"

"Wonderful!" The old man concluded his presentation. "So you see there are many ways by which, and many shores from which, to arrive in these United States. Unless you are American Indian, or your ancestors were brought here as slaves, everyone's story is essentially the same. We fled persecution or instability or poverty or simple lack of freedom to come here in pursuit of a better life."

"Great," muttered Stella, "now that I've died of embarrassment."

"Most people started out poor and worked their way up. People tried all sorts of things when they moved here! This wagon symbolizes only one type of experience. Notably, this young lady's family's," he said, nodding at Eileen who took it as a compliment and jutted out her chin.

"Students," called Ms. Queen from across the room, "come see the printing presses. Now this is a symbol of status." The young social studies teacher looked intently at Stella, who wondered, why am I invisible when I don't want to be — and stared at when I want to be alone?

The elderly volunteer crossed the room and began lining up letters in the archaic black iron printing press. There was ink everywhere! Now Stella understood why he wore the apron. Into Stella's mind flooded images and questions. Her mother told her stories when they cooked Sunday dinners, about grandfather dressing in traditional Korean costume. As Stella remembered, it had a simple, clean front, like the old man's apron. Her grandfather had been a scholar in Korea. He sat at a desk with a paintbrush and a printing stamp, writing in calligraphy and signing it with a carved stamp by candlelight.

". . . the American alphabet is simple, of course, but this press required that the letters be placed upside-down . . ."

And then during the war, Stella remembered, something happened, and her grandfather began using a press . . . She thought this was right. She wondered whether he had needed to earn money, but that didn't seem right, either. Mother said later that his robes became soiled, his calligraphy ignored. Somehow, the calligraphy was connected to their family's emigration.

". . . during war-time presses were a prime target of the enemy, because, the Americans would print notices to support the war. It was the chief way of communicating. The pen, as they say, is mightier than the sword."

And then. . . Stella remembered that he was gone. He must have died. She wondered why her mother lost her father when she was so young, why her Grandmother was widowed.

Stella looked up at the old man, not hearing a word he said and remembered. Grandfather was killed during the war. That's what father said in response to her persistent questions. Her mother was too sensitive, too easily hurt, for Stella to pester her about this part of the story. Grandmother shouted at her and told her to wait until she was old enough to understand. It had something to do with Communists.

Stella looked closely at the old man running the press. She looked at his wrinkled hands, his cheerful manner, his skillful operation of the press. Her grandfather must have been just like this man: cheerful, intelligent, and kind. Like Albert, she thought. He must also have been tough when things became difficult during the war. He must have been mad. Mad and tough. Like Frankie. Like Grandmother and father. But no — she wondered how one person could change so much. Maybe he was . . . She frowned and swallowed. Maybe she was a little like him, too.

Soon, their visit was over. The students filed out into the high afternoon sun, along with students from the other schools. It was strange. The Chicago girls seemed older, with teased hair and black eyeliner, and the boys seemed younger, smaller, and more fragile. These students looked like they themselves may have flown or walked into this country. The ancestors of some had to have been slaves. Their bus said Walt Disney Magnet School. "City kids look older," commented Rachel, as they climbed up the stairs onto their own bus.

Eileen looked back over her shoulder at the groups of smiling, shy students. "Trash," she said. "Probably all on drugs. Or in gangs. That's what my mother says. Probably," Eileen said, smiling sweetly over her shoulder at a lovely dark-haired, dark-eyed girl wearing a white turtleneck, "parents already." Eileen spit the last words out at her friends with a harsh, small laugh. Stella's stomach began to knot. She angrily looked at Eileen. The dark-haired girl was looking at Eileen with hurt eyes. Stella smiled at the dark-haired girl, who smiled back and waved. Stella, standing back in the cold wind waiting to get on the bus, looked back at Eileen, who smiled at her expectantly. Taking a big step up to the bus, Stella paused on the stairs and just looked at the city kids, who were Asian or Latino or Black. For once, she didn't smile back at Eileen.

Chapter 7

Trying On Clothes

"What did you get, Stella?"

Eileen peered over Jesse's shoulder, mouth pursed in a fake little smile. Jesse's huge feet rested on the seat in front of him. He deliberately folded a piece of paper.

"Well, Stella?"

Stella smiled a bit at the rounded numbers on her paper. The "9" was so fat; it looked like a bulb on a stick. The "5" was so cute; it looked like a pregnant lady in a hat.

"It's almost time for the announcements," said Mrs. Factor, the math teacher, "write down tomorrow's assignment. By the way, it's rude to compare scores!" The teacher sat at her desk and began grading papers.

"Stella!" Eileen's hand rested on Jesse's desk. He didn't seem to notice. Stella turned her paper over and leaned back on her chair. She and Rachel exchanged smiles. It was sunny out today.

"Jesse got a 97! Is that what you got?"

A cloud passed over the sun, and Stella grimaced. She punched the desk with her fist.

"It's not fair," she said to Rachel, and glowered. "He never studies. I studied for two weeks for that stupid test." She crumpled her paper in her hands and pouted. Into her mind flew an image of the dry cleaning store and her father with a frustrated face. She pouted angrily. "Now he'll really be disappointed," she muttered.

In the meantime, Rachel turned to Eileen and asked, "Hey, Eileen, what did you get on the test? 100?"

Eileen shrugged her shoulders. "I got a 78. Who cares?" Stella raised her eyebrow and turned around.

"How could she get such a low grade when I helped her?" she said to herself.

A reedy, clipped voice sailed in from the hallway. "I want the rules distributed promptly, so that the competition will be eminently fair." Stella's pout faded. She glanced toward the voice. A long, azure-blue suited stick-shaped woman stood just outside the doorway. Eileen jerked her hand from Jesse's desk and folded her test with shaking hands. It wrinkled when she shoved it into the pocket of her binder. Rachel watched Eileen nervously push her hair back from her face.

"Yes, Mrs. Englehart," came Dr. Drummond's voice, "they

have been copied and will be distributed today. There is no need for concern . . ."

"I hope that you will distribute them promptly!" Mrs. Englehart said in dismissal. The principal hurried away. Stella slumped back into her chair.

When the announcements barked through the loudspeaker, Eileen almost jumped out of her seat. The students sat still for a moment to listen:

"Don't forget that the 25th annual spelling bee will be held on April 22nd, less than three weeks from today. You should already have your books. Those of you who plan to enter must master the introductory list before Monday's meeting, when the rule sheets will be available. Sign-up sheets for the competition will be available from any of your teachers."

Mrs. Englehart poked her head in the classroom and hunted for Eileen. Although she did this regularly, every time, she seemed not to know where Eileen's seat was. "Hello, darling!" she said to Eileen, who got out of her chair and walked toward her mother. From her seat near the door, Stella heard them speak.

"I got a B on the math test, Mom," lied Eileen.

"Yes, that's nice, dear."

"See you for dinner, Mom?"

"Ah, of course, dear," smiled Mrs. Englehart, her cold eyes sparkling against the sea-blue fabric she wore. She seemed to look at something just over Eileen's head. Eileen stood closer to her and looked up.

"Can we plan my party today, mom?"

Her mother nodded absently.

When Eileen noticed that her friends in the corner were watching, she flipped her hair back, jerked her shoulders, and stepped back from her mom. "Okay, I'm getting the spelling bee stuff today, Mom," she said. For the first time her mother focused her eyes completely on her daughter.

"See that you do." As Eileen pushed past the other students in line for the sign-up sheet, Mrs. Englehart left. When she arrived at Mrs. Factor's desk, Eileen turned around, and noticed that her mother was gone. She stood with two sheets in her hand, watching the door. She turned to Stella.

"Here, Stella," Eileen smiled, though her eyes looked sad, "do you want to come over today after school? I think my mom has a meeting, so it'll just be the two of us."

Stella realized that Rachel wasn't invited. Amanda and Eileen's other friends watched from the back. They weren't invited, either. Rachel seemed to be thinking about something else.

"Well, then, just meet me out front where Rose picks me up!" Eileen tossed her head and returned to her seat where she whispered to Amanda and Heather. When they giggled, Stella's skin tingled and she sat up. She looked at the group yearningly, as she sat outside of it, as usual. Trying not to believe that they were laughing at her, she looked back and forth in confusion and then shrugged, resigned to following Eileen's plans. Nothing she did mattered anyway. She frowned in annoyance when a paper airplane sailed over her shoulder. It was Jesse's near-perfect test which he had thrown at her. "Nothing like rubbing it in," she said, and refused to look at him.

❦

It was only 3:30 when Rose pulled the Englehart's black Volvo into the garage. Eileen gossiped about Amanda and Heather to Stella. As she stepped from the garage into the bright clean kitchen, Stella inhaled deeply. There was no scent, and everything looked so clear. Stella inhaled again with satisfaction.

Rose made the girls a snack of brie cheese and Cheerios, Eileen's favorite. As the girls picked at the Cheerios, Eileen asked, "Is Mom home yet?"

Rose shook her head and looked at the girl with searching eyes before answering, "No, darlin'. Your mama's gone to a meetin'."

"Oh," Eileen said softly. Her eyes looked open and hurt. Then she threw her shoulders back and said, "Who cares?"

She started talking about all her friends. She told Stella about Amanda getting caught cutting class. She talked about meeting Jesse at the bookstore in the mall. She talked about everything, it seemed, except the upcoming birthday party. Stella politely forced down the rich, bitter-tasting cheese. Her fingers were sticky with it. When their conversation began to run down, Stella said, "Do you want to start with the spelling words now?"

"Well," responded Eileen, leaning forward with her pointed chin resting on her hand, "I wanted to ask you something."

"Yes?" Stella sat up, leaning forward hopefully.

"Well, I think," Eileen paused, smiled shyly at Stella, and giggled, "we should enter the spelling bee together! Then you could . . . we could do the work and go to the meetings together!"

Her head slightly lowered, Stella said, "Sure." Her insides froze at the thought, but she slid off the stool and pulled the book of spelling words out of her backpack.

"I'm sick of work," said Eileen. Stella looked at her in confusion. She couldn't understand what Eileen wanted.

Stella nodded her head, ready to agree to anything, desperate for the invitation.

"I know," said Eileen, "let's. . . dress up!"

"With what? With dolls?" Stella was confused. Everything changed so quickly with Eileen.

Eileen just smiled slyly and dropped the uneaten brie on her plate. "Let's go," she said, pulling the sleeve of Stella's green sweater.

The girls raced up the curving, wide wooden stairs. She

followed her friend into the Engleharts' bedroom. It seemed private, and Stella frowned. Yet Eileen ran through the airy blue-carpeted room toward the dressing area just past the bed. She held open the door and said, "Come on, slowpoke!" Stella rubbed her fingers together, trying to wipe off the brie.

The closet was as big as Stella's Grandmother's bedroom. Cold light filtered in through the small high window, allowing the girls to see the bright-colored clothes hanging before them. They stood silently for a minute. Eileen moved first.

Dresses flew off their hangers, scarves tumbled from their racks, and sweaters fell off their shelf. The rough wool, pearly buttons, and fluid silk hung from their thin shoulders and pulled over their thin blond and thick dark hair. Eileen was modeling a cocktail dress, when Stella looked up from her struggle with a difficult zipper.

"Just pull on it!" Eileen said, but Stella was worried that it would break. Before she could look up, a transparent gold lame jacket was thrown on her head. Stella forgot the zipper and just pulled up the skirt. The two girls, cramping with laughter, pushed past each other and struggled to look in the long, narrow mirror fastened to the closet door.

The neckline on Eileen's black dress plunged to the middle of her stomach. Mrs. Englehart was a tall woman. It looked ridiculous. Stella wobbled on red spike heels, clutched the gray pleated skirt under her arms and poked her head through the golden jacket. What a look!

Although the sun was fading, its orange rays illuminated the teal blues, mocha browns, and iridescent whites in the clothes. The girls' reflections shone, and they felt swept up in a dream. The colors had a biting hue to them in the late afternoon sun.

Stella remembered Rachel, who loved to pretend and play with clothes. Standing now in a deep brown sweaterdress draped with a pink scarf, Stella imagined Rachel playing too, adding a belt to Eileen's dress, tying Stella's scarf, always adding ideas and fun. It seemed stupid that all three of them couldn't be friends.

Stella's smile slid off her face as she wondered whether she could belong here. These glamorous, expensive clothes would always be too long for her, no matter how old she got.

Eileen was squirming as she tried to button the back of a purple velvet dress. Her voice jolted Stella.

"Hey! Help! I'm . . . we're going to the . . . school board ball! Get a sitter, Rose. This party is the most important thing in the universe!" Her voice had an edge to it. Her eyes glinted angrily.

Stella helped her friend push the fat, velvet-covered buttons into the petite, perfect buttonholes.

Eileen pulled away so abruptly that the button hole ripped. She danced a circle by herself, imitating her parents. Stella's arm was pulled roughly as Eileen started to dance with her.

"My darling," Eileen said, "you really must close the merger before breakfast. Otherwise, how shall we leave to ski?"

Stella smiled warily. Then, Eileen's long, lacy sleeve caught on a hanger which the girls had earlier thrown aside. She jerked her arm and the cloth tore farther. It seemed almost deliberate. Stella's spine stiffened at the sound.

Eileen waltzed without stopping.

"What are you . . .?"

"Oh, who cares," Eileen replied. "Rose just takes it to the cleaners. It's their job to fix it, right?"

In Stella's mind flashed a picture of her pretty mother, hunched over the old metal machine in the musty store, wearing cheap polyester pants and a button-up blouse. Even Rose dressed better than her mother did.

"My mother's a nurse!" Stella blurted out to Eileen's back as her friend pulled at the delicate clothing.

"So? I knew that. Who cares?" said Eileen, distracted now by a different dress.

"Anyway, my mother doesn't work like yours does. She stays home with me," Eileen spoke fiercely, standing stock-still in the middle of her mother's closet.

"But she's never here!"

Tears glinted in Eileen's eyes. Stella covered her mouth when she realized what she had said, but it was too late. Something like revenge sparkled in Eileen's eyes.

"Who cares what your mom does!" Eileen ripped another

seam almost on purpose as she stepped out of her dress. "What's so great about your mom? She's never home, either! I haven't been at your house for so long that I don't even know what she does!" Eileen was practically screaming now. "She's probably not even a nurse!"

"I have to go." Despite her anger, Stella carefully pulled off the gold lame jacket and winced at the sight of the heap of clothes on the floor.

"No way! We didn't study yet! I have to win the . . . That's why I invit . . . ." Eileen bit her lip angrily, trying to control herself. "You have to stay for dinner!"

Stella walked out of the closet and through the bedroom.

"I can't believe . . . you're just ignoring me!" Eileen planted her hands on her hips and flipped her hair. Stella stepped out of the bedroom. The sky was still light outside the windows. Spring was coming. With a different tone of voice, Eileen said, "Wait! Okay, wait." She ripped the hem as she stepped out of the dress, "Rose will take you, and we'll practice the words in the car."

"No. I just want to walk," Stella said as she stepped down the stairs. Eileen's voice seemed different, softer. Despite herself, Stella still felt a closeness to her. "Thanks for everything," Stella said softly. In the kitchen, Stella said goodbye to Rose and hoisted up her backpack. She opened the door. As she stepped out into the late afternoon, she heard Eileen calling.

"But I entered you in the contest already! You have to help me! You have to!" It was the same old voice. Stella walked away from the house.

❦

As Stella opened their water-streaked storm door, it scraped against the sagging concrete. Her face was flushed from walking fast in the chilled, late-winter air. She stubbed her toe on the doorjamb and looked down. By her foot, a soiled cigarette butt poked out of a wasted little snowpile. Nothing was what it seemed, she thought. Clean snow hid dirt. Friendship hid meanness. She finally slammed the front door open and threw her backpack against the couch. She was sick of fakes. After changing her clothes, she walked downstairs and challenged the boys to a soccer match. Albert and Frankie looked at each other, told Stella they would play, and then laughed wildly together. Curious, Stella followed them outside.

The kicking and the bracing cold air felt good. Stella's sweatshirt and jeans got muddy and wet, her wild hair flew as she chased and slammed the ball with her feet. She had to play extra hard against the two boys. She always played on a team by herself.

When she came back from retrieving the ball from the neighbor's yard, Stella didn't see Frankie. Fine, she thought, now she could catch her breath. Albert was an easy opponent. Stella dribbled easily past her brother two or three times and then stopped abruptly. She put her hands on her hips and said, "Why are you giving these away? It isn't any fun when you quit on me!" Albert pushed his hair from his forehead and grinned. He looked really skinny and small to Stella today, but she knew that he was growing. "What's going on?" She looked around again for Frankie.

Albert suddenly disappeared around the side of the house. Stella, frustrated, picked up the ball and followed him. She wasn't going to get a good game out of them today, she realized. Then she stopped dead in her tracks when she saw her brother Frankie.

He was standing on the steps by the side door, wearing his dirty coat and shoes, but in his mouth was a cigarette and on his face were grandmother's glasses. Stella's jaw dropped open in surprise. "You're too young to smoke, you idiot. Where did you get Apba's cigarette?" Albert stood to the side and giggled, while Frankie slowly pushed the smeary plastic glasses up his nose. When Stella didn't react, he took them off and began cleaning them with his scarf.

"What are you doing with Grandmother's glasses?"

"It's not just her glasses, Smella!" said Frankie, grinning. Albert hopped back and forth, virtually exploding with laughter. Stella's eyebrows lifted and her lips widened in a smile.

"No. No way. That isn't hers."

"Yes, way! Yes, way!" said Albert, finally letting his laughter overcome him. He clutched his sides and leaned over.

"Grandmother smokes? How do you know?" Stella was astonished. Korean women didn't smoke. Grandmother always lectured her about behaving properly. She couldn't break the rules. Suddenly, the side door began to pull open. Frankie ran off like a shot. Albert hid against the side of the house, leaving Stella, filthy and astonished, to face her Grandmother.

"Sung Ok!" The door was opened, and Grandmother stood blinking inside of it. "Have you seen my glasses?"

❧

At the sink after dinner, Stella dried while Grandmother washed. Her brothers were watching T.V. downstairs, and her parents were still at work. Stella looked forward to tomorrow, when she would spend the whole day with them again.

"You must obey," said her Grandmother in English. Stella had no idea what Grandmother was talking about. She was obeying her Grandmother. "Obey man," said Grandmother, scrubbing the old black frying pan. Stella rolled her eyes. She wondered how Grandmother could possibly think Stella would follow this.

"Man is boss."

Stella wondered if her Grandmother kept the cigarettes in her apron pocket . . . Stella leaned back, trying to peek.

"Father rules mother."

"Mother doesn't mind it, but . . ." Stella's words bounced around inside her head as her Grandmother continued to speak.

"Mother rules family."

"That's not true, Grandmother. You rule this family. You don't follow these rules yourself! Why should I follow them?" Stella was surprised at herself for speaking up.

"You must obey man, for dignity and happiness."

"You Grandmothers at church rule everything! The men sit together smoking while you make all the decisions!" All Stella could think about was the bashed-in cigarette hanging from Frankie's little mouth. She struggled to keep her face clear, but she was losing the battle.

"When you marry, your husband will support you. Your job is to make son, make home."

"But Grandmother, you don't have a son . . ." ventured Stella. What happened next stunned Stella. Grandmother actually stopped working, and two small tears drifted down the sides of her nose where her glasses usually were. She put down the soapy sponge and walked out of the room.

Stella felt afraid to follow her Grandmother to the laundry room. Maybe she needed to be alone. In a short time, Grandmother came back and continued, as if there had been no interruption.

"Women's accomplishments don't matter," Grandmother

said. "School is important, but it doesn't matter to woman's real life. Your calling in life is to serve the family," Grandmother barely paused in soaping the sinkful of pots and pans. Stella watched her closely, to see if she felt alright. Grandmother looked away from Stella when she said, "Especially if weak like you, Sung Ok. Must follow man. No spirit in self." Stella's spirit exploded, she couldn't control her face or her voice.

"So why do I study three or four hours a day? No one else studies as hard as I do. Why should I bother, if I'm just a worthless girl?" Stella's words came faster as she got angrier. "Why did you send Mama to nursing school — and after the war, when you were so poor? What's the point? Why does Apba yell at me about homework every day? And what's the big deal about me doing so well in math?"

"You serve as example for your brothers. They will be our family's success."

"That's just stupid!"

Stella felt Grandmother shoving a pan at her. The clouds just hung in the sky through the small, square kitchen window. Grandmother was still talking. The pan was dripping soapy water on her sock. Grandmother didn't wash well without her glasses. The sky was black and gray. Stella looked away and hiccuped.

"I'm just working for them? What about myself? What about my dreams? This is America! You can't treat me like that here!

I'm not some stupid slave!"

Stella was drying rapidly, efficiently, and mechanically. For the first time in her life, she totally ignored her Grandmother. If she had listened, she would have heard her Grandmother complimenting her work.

"I'll be a professor like Rachel's mom!" she practically yelled at last. "You can't make me follow bozos like those two idiot brothers I have! I'll show you!"

Stella was so angry that she didn't notice her Grandmother's smile. Her eyes glinted with satisfaction as her granddaughter huffed and turned her back. The old woman sensed the girl's growing power.

❦

Stella was in her room studying when her parents came home. She ran down the stairs to the living room to greet them but as usual, her father shooed her away so that he could eat in peace. Her mother looked exhausted. Stella felt angry that her father wouldn't allow her to help her mom. Sometimes, she felt pushed away by their Korean ways.

Her math homework was done perfectly like her Apba wanted, and she had given the answers to Eileen over the phone. Even though her stomach hurt, at least she didn't have to worry about what might happen on Monday. She looked at her nightstand, and noticed that Frankie had left Grandmother's glasses there. She had no idea how to return them. Stella felt pressured and confused, so she escaped into a daydream.

In the dream, her parents had their professional jobs again, and her mother came home every day at three o'clock, the way she used to. But Stella was older, and more confident, and Eileen came over all the time. She imagined Eileen looking at Stella's clothes and envying them. She would lend some clothes to Eileen, who would feel grateful. Then she looked around her warm room again and realized that reality was very different.

She was looking over the blue spelling booklet. The intermediate words weren't too hard. She reflected for a moment. Leaving Eileen's house yesterday wasn't too hard, either. Language Arts wasn't any harder than math. It was easier, in fact. Stella realized something surprising. Eileen wasn't any smarter than she was. She leaned over her spelling words and began seriously studying.

Stella was rubbing her eyes when the door slid open. It was Grandmother. She laid a platter of corn tea and fruit on Stella's desk and turned to go. Then Grandmother noticed her glasses and walked over to pick them up. On her way out, she stopped to ask, "Where did you find my glasses?"

Hiding Behind Mother

"Well, Mrs. Kim, enjoy the rest of your weekend!" Mrs. Ontkean, the pharmacist from the next door store, waved. On the counter was a plate of muffins she had left.

Mrs. Kim smiled and shook her head. "That lady is too kind," she said to Stella. "Remind me to bring her something next Saturday!" Stella agreed and carried the plate of muffins to the card table in the middle of the store. It would be perfect for their next break. They were having a good day. Stella had forgotten all about her frustrations with Eileen and her Grandmother from the day before. She even managed to put the spelling bee and the birthday party out of her mind. Well, almost. She glanced at her pile of books on the counter and decided to study a little between customers.

Around three o'clock, her mom was in the back helping her Apba finish some cleaning with the dark, heavy machinery, and

Stella was minding the front as usual. Spring is finally here, Stella thought with a smile as she looked out the window. Her smile suddenly slid off her face. There, in front of the plate glass window, was Mrs. Englehart getting out of her black Volvo wagon and hoisting a bag full of laundry out of the passenger seat. Stella was confused, because she thought that Rose took the clothes in, and that they went to the other store in town. Then Stella remembered that Rose had the weekend off because of her niece's wedding.

She gripped the counter with her hands so hard that her knuckles stuck out. "I can't wait on her, I can't," she whispered to herself, and she whipped her body around, thick hair flying behind her, and practically dove into a pile of clothes behind the counter.

Grabbing a couple of shirts from the pile, and purposely pulling off their tags, she hurried back to the machines where her parents were and looked at them, bright-eyed, half out of breath, "Is this the shirt belonging to Mr. Jones? Is it? I'm not sure, I'm just not sure. You see, this tag just fell off. If it's his, then maybe you need it now. Mom, I'll take this to the right pile now. Someone is at the door. You get it, Mom. I'll be over here!" Stella kept walking as she talked. She was now close to the basement steps.

"What are you doing? Are you crazy? That tag was right there," said her mother. "It was right on the shirt. You put it on yourself. I'm busy helping your father. Open your eyes!" Mother turned back to her work.

The bell rang at the front counter, the little round one with the white index card taped in front of it that said "ring for service." Stella could just imagine what Eileen would say, "There's old 'ling for service!' Herro! Chopsticks, ponytail. Garlic breath. Chinese, Chinese!" She saw how they made fun of In Sook Chang's accent. In Sook had just moved to America last year. Stella wasn't anything like her. It was so unfair. Everything made her so angry lately.

"There's a customer in front! Stella, go wait on her."

"Excuse me, hello?" said Mrs. Englehart. Ring, ring, ring, chimed the bell.

"Stella! Go up front!!"

I can't, I can't! "Mom! You wait on her!" said Stella. Her mother's sharp tone shocked Stella.

"Sung Ok, I said wait on her. Go to the front and wait on her."

Stella whispered, "No, no, Mama. I can't. Why did you quit your job? Why do you do everything Apba says? I hate this stupid store!" She ran into the bathroom. Stella, over the running water, could hear her mother rushing up to the front and taking Mrs. Englehart's order. Mrs. Englehart sounded sarcastic and annoyed. "She couldn't have heard me," muttered Stella as she looked at herself in the mirror. Her eyes looked startled and her cheeks were flushed. She looked particularly pale. She took deep breaths to calm herself.

"If Eileen knew I worked here like a servant, cleaning her mother's clothes, she'd tell everyone. They'd all make fun of me. Why did Apba have to quit his job? He used to have a normal job. Why! Why!" She saw two spots of angry red on her cheeks now, replacing the embarrassed blush. Over the running water she wondered why she was so angry all the time. She didn't know what would happen next.

❧

Later that night, Stella's father came into her room.

"You hurt your mother's feelings," he said. "You were disobedient. There is no excuse for such language. Your sharpness wounds others." His voice was soft, but she could hear his anger. He looked at her sharply, but curiously also, with his brown-black eyes.

"I feel like I'm changing, Apba! I don't understand anything!" She looked at him carefully as he considered what she said.

"Apologize to your mother," said her father, "and obey her. You must behave. You are becoming too American." Stella listened silently, worried about what this might mean.

"Your Grandmother is right about you. Maybe it is time for you to go to Korean school. Maybe you will spend this summer in Korea. You must not grow up wild." Stella's thoughts flashed around wildly.

"But if I go to Korean school, then I can't help at the store!"

She knew that this made no sense, in light of her actions that day. She looked up at her father again, her eyes like a child's.

"You never talk to your mother like that. She is crying."

Stella felt afraid, worried and confused. She looked up at her Apba with her pretty wet eyes, and said, "I'm sorry, Apba, I'm sorry."

"Just obey your mother; you must treat your parents with respect," and then quietly left the room and shut the door. Stella wondered how she was supposed to know how to act. The other kids didn't have to worry about acting too American. Everything was harder for her.

Stella looked around her room and saw pictures of Great America, rock stars, and her favorite Valentine kitten poster. Her favorite books lined a shelf above the desk her parents had gotten her when she started fifth grade. On the bulletin board next to the desk were her pictures and keepsakes, including a little soccer ball keychain, a ribbon for running fastest in her grade last year, and in the corner, a ticket stub to Great America from last year and a picture of her there with Eileen. The program from the symphony that Eileen's family had taken her to hung below the ticket stub.

She looked at the floor and saw her Korean chest. Inside were her colorful formal clothes and a crown that her mother wore at her wedding. In mother's chest were many of the same things, and some special family jewelry as well, which would become Stella's when she grew up. Some day, mother's jewelry would go in Stella's dark lacquer jewelry box covered with shiny white flowers and birds. That day felt impossibly far away. She knew that she was acting like a baby, but at the same time, she knew that eventually she would get the gold necklace. In her Korean life, she knew what would happen. It made her feel safe.

Her room was Korean, too, different from her friends' rooms, but full of things she loved. The dried tears pulled on Stella's cheek. Her mother must be feeling sad, too. Maybe she would just give up trying to be like everyone else, so that she wouldn't be so mean. After sitting quietly in her room for another moment, Stella went downstairs to find her mother.

Chapter 9

A Glimpse of Apba's World

The slamming door shook the house. Blinking her eyes, Stella rolled over sleepily to look at the clock.

The glowing orange face said two-thirty. She shook her foggy head. "Am I late?" she wondered aloud in the darkness. "Where's Mom?"

She pulled herself into a sitting position. The warm covers fell from her shoulders; the air was chilly. The darkness was unrelieved, except for the orange glow and the crack of light under the bedroom door. Her mother must be asleep downstairs.

She remembered that it was Sunday, Apba's regular soccer night. It surprised her that she would feel this disoriented after two hours of sleep. The day's memories came back to her: spending most of the day at church, cooking dinner with her mother, studying throughout the evening. The darkness faded into a kind of relief, and she was able to make out some shapes in her room. A shadowy thin book lay on the floor. The tray of fruit and crackers lay on her low red table.

She heard another light clicking on downstairs. An outburst of yelling shattered the quiet. It was Apba.

When Mother responded, he just talked louder. She felt tense. Stella sat bolt upright, and her feet slid slowly into her slippers. She tiptoed to her door and slid it open.

All in Korean, her father was shouting, "those —— kicked out every single Asian in the place! We were just playing a damn soccer game! A soccer game!" Something slammed against the wall. Stella imagined her father's hand balled into a fist. She shivered in fear and cold — she wore only a thin cotton nightgown — but crept quietly to the top of the stairs.

"I'm late because I had to bail Bong Kyu Lee out of jail!" Stella knew Mr. Lee. His daughter, Nora, was Stella's friend at church. They lived in Chicago, near Koreatown and had an electronics store. Stella had seen Mr. Lee yell before, but she never knew that he was a criminal.

By now, she was perched behind the wrought-iron railing at the top of the steps. If they had looked, her parents could have seen her. Mother sat calmly on the couch, watching her husband pace restlessly. Despite his movements, she was quiet. He began to tell the story.

"We were playing a Greek or Italian team. The nationality

doesn't matter. What matters is that the referee was the same nationality as the other team. We were winning 4-3 in the last quarter. If we won this game, we were sure to go to the championship. Then the ref started making every call against us. It was ridiculous. He was kicking our players out of the game, giving the other side penalty kicks. Even the crowd was booing him. It was so obviously unfair."

Stella was stunned that they could do this to her Apba. She wondered if it was because he was Korean. She lit up with anger, but felt a little frightened at the same time. It seemed like these had to be important people, to be able to treat someone that way. Nevertheless, it confused her that such a thing could happen.

"Then we stopped playing and protested. We got into an argument with the referee, and the manager of the league came out. The referee kicked our best players out of the game, so we'd have no chance for the championship. By this time the crowd was yelling at him, but he did it anyway."

"And then that —— manager kicked us out of the league. What a ——! For protesting about unfair calls! They were clearly discriminating. So Bong Kyu stupidly kicked the ball at the score board. We told him to calm down and stop it, that he wasn't solving anything. The manager called the police, and got him arrested. I couldn't believe it! Tempers always get hot at soccer games! You don't go arresting somebody!"

Although she sat silently in her robe, hands clasped in her lap, Stella's mother radiated strength as she listened to her husband. His voice cut the silence of the night; his wife's silence was like water, washing calmness over his fury. Stella felt surprised to be drawn more toward her mother than her father. He hadn't yet taken off his sweat pants and jacket. His dirty cleats lay by the door.

"So we went together to the jail and contributed money to bail him out. I paid $100." Stella's Mother nodded. Mr. Lee had to run his store tomorrow, too. Friends from church supported one another. Her father paused and looked his wife full in the face. Stella was startled by their intensity; she had never seen such emotion between them. In front of Stella and her brothers, her parents acted more like business partners than anything else.

"He went home, and the rest of us went back to the stadium to watch the last game and talk about what happened. We were standing aside drinking pops and talking, and then the manager appeared with a policeman and told us to leave or he'd have us all arrested. Arrested!"

Now he started pacing again. Stella clutched her knees to her chest. She couldn't leave. Behind her in the dark hallway, everything was still.

"That's when Mr. Kwon spoke up," her father continued, "You know Mr. Kwon. He works downtown in a law firm and plays soccer with us every week. He told the manager that he was a lawyer, and that he wanted to know what the charge would be. The manager didn't believe he was a lawyer, so they argued. Finally, the manager believed him, but he stuck to his decision to kick us out of the stadium for no reason. He said the charge would be criminal trespass, because this was private property."

"Mr. Kwon was angry, and he told us to decide ourselves whether to leave or not. He said that although the stadium was private property, it was open to the public. We had every right to be there like anyone else. He told this manager that he would sue him for racial discrimination. He said, 'I'll make you make some lawyer rich,' and the manager looked scared. He stuck to his decision and not only kicked us out, he went through the crowd with the policeman and ordered every Asian person to leave. If you were a Filipino sitting in the crowd to watch a Greek friend, you got kicked out, too! We all decided to leave, even though they had no right to kick us out. We couldn't afford to be arrested, rightfully or wrongly."

Her Apba finally sat on the couch. Stella, afraid that they would notice her, pulled her legs back up off the stairs and scooted back into the hallway. She could no longer see them, but she could hear everything. Her heart clutched with anger and fear that someone treated her Apba like that. The world seemed to loom like a mysterious shadow; it was a place where her father could not always protect her.

There was no more talking. Eventually, the refrigerator door was pulled open. The sound was faintly reassuring. Stella rose to her feet and stepped softly into her dark room. She stood just inside the doorway in the darkness, wondering what step she could take. The deep, soft shadows pushed in on her. She felt that she couldn't rest.

She flicked on the light. Her mathbook lay open. The work was complete. She struggled to achieve in math for her father's sake, but it didn't seem to make things any better. The spelling book lay closed. She held the flimsy book between her hands and wondered why she worked so hard. Winning the spelling bee couldn't solve these problems. She glanced briefly over the word lists but then put the booklet away and turned off the light. The house was completely silent. Stella felt like she held some family secrets. Somehow, she would help make things right.

Pushed Around

Stella walked alone to the cafeteria. Eileen was getting help from Mrs. Factor and probably from Jesse, too. Stella couldn't believe that Eileen stopped calling her for answers after Jesse got a higher grade on last Monday's test. She felt empty and relieved at the same time. Eileen would want help with the spelling bee. She was working hard, just so that she could help Eileen, she told herself. Stella couldn't care less about Jesse; Rachel was his friend.

She couldn't believe that only a week had passed since April Fool's. Although the spelling bee was in exactly two weeks, Stella tried not to think about it. In a short span of time, she was learning things that she never wanted to know

Rachel wanted to meet Stella today to talk about the spelling bee. As she walked toward the cafeteria door, sniffing to discover what lunch would be today, something knocked her off her feet and against the lockers. The cold metal rammed her shoulder, and her books tumbled all over the floor. A group of boys ran down the hall.

"What the . . ." she said, angry but shaking. She leaned over to clean up her books, and by the sound of huge pounding, gym-shoed feet, realized that the boys were coming by again. Bronko and his friends were running through the halls and shoving people to see if they would fall. Stella grabbed her books in a messy pile and shoved the heavy swinging door to the girls' room before they could get her again. It flew open, and she rushed in.

Shaken, Stella stood in the bathroom and remembered the last time Bronko chased her. Her books lay forgotten on the wet formica around the sinks. In the mirror, she noticed that her face was pale, as it had been the day that Mrs. Englehart came into their store. She shook her head to push the images away, but a different memory emerged in her mind's eye instead.

One day two years ago, when she and Eileen were still best friends, these same boys had chased her at recess. Stella leaned against the bathroom counter as she thought. At first, all she could remember was one phrase:

❧

"Chinese, Japanese, dirty knees, look at these!" they had yelled, pulling out their shirts in two points at the chest. At first it was just Richard Jones, but then his two friends joined him. Bronko started chasing her in circles, and as Stella ran, they pursued her further and further from Ms. Queen. She found herself surrounded by five boys, standing against the wall. She shook now at the very memory.

A familiar voice screamed out from behind Richard Jones' head. Bronko was so startled that he turned around. Stella inched out of the circle, sensing a chance to escape. "Get out of there! You idiots!"

The boys quieted and turned to face Rachel. She was approaching the group alone, but something about her seemed big and powerful. Her long hair blew in the wind, and her blue-green eyes were fearless. The skin on Stella' s elbow scraped against the bricks as she squirmed her way out of the circle. The bell rang, signaling the five-minute warning. The boys looked up. In the confusion, Rachel shouted, "Dr. Drummond is coming!"

The boys scattered. Before they could realize what happened, Rachel put her arm around Stella. The girls ran, laughing toward the school door.

"Thanks," Stella whispered, as Rachel guided her back towards Ms. Queen. Then she looked around. "Where's Dr. Drummond?"

"Oh, I don't know," replied Rachel, holding her head high and keeping an arm on Stella as they passed the group of boys, now talking among themselves and pointing at Rachel. They realized now that Dr. Drummond wasn't even outside. Rachel had fooled them.

"Why did you help me?"

"Oh, because they're stupid idiots," Rachel said. The girls started laughing as they left the boys behind. From that moment onward, they were friends.

❦

Standing at the bathroom sink, Stella saw that the color had returned to her face. If they push me, then I'll just push back, she decided. She grabbed her books under her arm. "Maybe I'll fight for myself from now on," she said to the face in the mirror, which began to sparkle with pride, "and maybe I'll just compete." As she kicked open the door, she reflected that there might be more to friendship than popularity.

Chapter 11

Charlie Chan, Part II

Saturday morning at the store, Stella was working hard to help her parents. The spelling bee was just over a week away, but it didn't matter. Stella wasn't going to compete. Nevertheless, she couldn't believe that a week had passed so quickly. There was a lot of work to do, but it was important to be with her parents today. She wasn't quite sure why.

Her father had circles under his eyes. Somehow, he seemed older. She didn't know what was bothering him so much, because he rarely spoke, but she had a guess.

Her mother struggled to hide her fatigue by splashing water on her face, but when no one was looking, Stella could see her wincing and rubbing her wrists. There was more to this family than met the eye.

Stella hoisted a pile of soiled work-shirts away from the glass-topped counter. There was so much to do, her parents seemed to need her so much. The weight settled around her with the heaviness of water pressing against her ribcage. She felt . . . she shook her head and bit her lip. She didn't know how she felt and wasn't sure it mattered.

When the doorbells tinkled, Stella saw Mr. Jones pushing the glass door open. He held two badly soiled workshirts. She stared at him. Stella finally recognized that he was Richard's dad from school.

"Hey, Charlie Chan! Howya doin'?" he yelled, before Stella's father could remove himself from Mr. Jones' presence. Before Stella and her mother could rush to the counter, her father had spun around. "Hey, how about some flied lice, Mrs. Chan?" said Mr. Jones, looking at Mrs. Kim. "I'll bet she's a good cook, eh, Charlie?" he said to Stella's father.

Her mother forced herself in front of Stella, and moved her body in such as way as to block her husband's view of Mr. Jones. Her movements were surprisingly powerful. "Yes, medium starch. By Tuesday will be okay? Thank you, Mr. Jones." She balled up the dirty shirts and pushed his arm away from the counter, to encourage him to leave. Two feet behind the counter stood Mr. Kim with clenched fists, glaring at the ignorant man.

"Hey, what's your hurry? I just wanted to say hello," he said with a frown, jerking his arm away from Mrs. Kim's gentle hand. He breathed in and looked around. "If you don't want my business . . ." he said, looking from Mrs. Kim to Mr. Kim. For a moment, it was silent. Then, Mr. Jones noticed Stella, standing off to the side with the order form.

"Yah, and that little girl has the book. How do I even know you took my order?" He frowned scornfully at Mrs. Kim. "Write it down." Stella flashed her eyes from the man to her mother, afraid of the expression she might find on her father's face. "Write it down, and . . . do it right."

"That is," he said, leaning across the counter and practically breathing on Mrs. Kim, "if that little gook knows how to write English." He stood up high and looked directly at Stella. "I've never even heard you speak, girl. What are you, mute? Or you just can't speak English like Papa-San over here?" He pointed at Mr. Kim with his index finger.

Mr. Jones didn't realize that you could only push Mr. Kim so far. Pointing directly at someone was practically an insult. Not knowing what would happen next, Stella forgot that she was standing in her parents' store until a red, tearing pain ripped through her abdomen. She bit her lip. In an effort to fight back the fear, she looked at her father with wide, soft eyes.

That was all that Mr. Kim needed. He pushed up the sleeves of his workshirt over his muscular forearms and focused on Mr. Jones. Stella's father walked forward to the counter and gently pushed his wife aside. In the meantime, Mr. Jones had stepped backward, closer to the door, looking nervously from side to side.

"Get out of store," Mr. Kim said, grabbing Mr. Jones' shirts from the countertop and walking around the side to the front of the store. Mr. Jones continued stepping backward, his pale eyes shining and his face sweating. He had nothing to say.

"Get out of store," said Mr. Kim, more softly now, although his voice was heated with rage. Mr. Jones backed out of the doorway, away from Mr. Kim. Mr. Jones tripped as he stepped downward onto the parking lot surface.

"Take your clothes and get out," said Mr. Kim, still advancing steadily with his smooth, athletic gait toward the taller, awkward, and frightened Mr. Jones. Mr. Kim raised his arm to throw the dirty clothes back at Mr. Jones, but he ducked and ran across the parking lot. His soiled ball of clothes lay on the wet asphalt.

Stella, still standing frozen behind the counter, watched as Mr. Jones ran toward his battered blue sedan at the far end of the parking lot and, without even a second glance toward the store or his abandoned clothes, jumped into the driver's seat and pulled out the entrance far from the store.

The drama ended. Mrs. Kim turned to her daughter.

"Wrap and put away Mrs. Ontkean's clothes, Sung Ok." Stella just stood there. "Sung Ok, go to the back of the store, now." Stella was not meant to hear what would be said between her parents next.

She walked to the back, all of her feelings yearning to be back with her parents. Because she was shaking, she sat down in hearing distance, still clutching the pharmacist's clothes. She knew that she wasn't supposed to be there. Even so, the yelling startled and upset her.

"To accept insults from garbage! Is that why we came here?" Mr. Kim stood with his wife in the front, heedless, for once, of speaking loudly in public. Stella sat quietly in the darkness. Fortunately, the mall was usually quiet at this time on Saturdays. Her stomach churned and churned. She felt that everything was spinning out of control. Her father might be arrested, too, like Mr. Lee.

"I gave up family. I gave up language. I gave up culture. I gave up even engineering in this country." Stella sat small in the darkness, trying to curl up and disappear. "At soccer, they arrest and insult us because we are Korean. Just because we are not white. We have dark hair. They kick us out!"

"Here, I clean other peoples' clothes. My wife gets illness," he said, probably picking up and looking at her swollen hands. Stella jerked in fear as her father slammed the front counter, knocking the cash register and felling some hangers. "They insult my child!" Stella was shaking even harder.

"My child! Am I polite to a man who insults my child! I cannot even support you here alone! My family must work and be broken by this culture along with me!" He was shouting.

Stella couldn't see up front, through the shadowy forest of hanging clothes between her seat and the counter, but she prayed that Mrs. Ontkean wouldn't hear. She curled up even tighter, even smaller.

"Bong Kyu was fined $1,000 by judge, sentenced to jail if he cannot pay. His crime is being Korean. That is the only reason police were called. He supports his mother in Korea. His brother's family lives with him. If he pays, he will not be able to pay rent on the store for one month. If he goes to jail for not paying, the store will close down."

There was another crash. Stella clenched her knees, afraid for her silent mother, who must be standing listening to Apba. Stella's thoughts raced like lightning. She was afraid for the store, and for her father. She had never heard him this angry before. It was as if he forgot everything else in the world.

"Even though I sacrifice, I try to make life better for my children. Bong Kyu tries to support his family. I give up engineering. He gives up college teaching. Sacrifice is acceptable when you give things up for a better way."

"But," he said, his words coming quickly but more softly now, in concentrated fury which was even more frightening than his screaming, "when discrimination makes sacrifice worthless, it is not acceptable."

"Too much," he continued softly, so softly that Stella could barely hear him. "Too much in this country is wrong." There was a long pause. Her mother said nothing. Stella felt angry that her mother was so silent. Stella's hands fell to her sides, and she pulled out of her clutched-up position to sit upright in her chair. She felt angry.

"Speak up, Mother!" she said to herself, louder now, "don't let him get so upset just because of one idiot!" She decided to tell them what a jerk Richard Jones was. That he had done the same thing to her before. Then they'd understand that it wasn't so serious.

She stopped halfway out of her seat. "Flied Lice." She remembered Eileen saying that to her in the hallway. Now Mr. Jones said it to her mother. She felt as if these people thought she was some kind of generic Oriental cartoon.

Her shoulders dropped as she paused to think about the words Rachel had used: discrimination, racism, and stereotypes. Maybe those were the words to describe what happened to her in school. Maybe that's what Eileen was doing. Her father screamed at Mr. Jones and chased him out. Stella wondered what she did to respond to such treatment.

Stella still followed Eileen. She obeyed her and gave her answers. She held back from competing so that Eileen could win. She went to her house. She tried to be like her, even though Eileen was so mean to her. Stella couldn't stand to think about it anymore. Maybe she should just fight . . . just compete . . . just win . . .

If she didn't follow Eileen, she would never be popular. She would just be some weirdo, some Korean geek girl who did well in math. She snorted in bitter laughter, as she sat thinking on the couch. "How typical," she said, "how stereotypical." Then Rachel's words came back to her: 'It's nice to surprise people, especially when they stereotype you.' Maybe she could surprise people by competing in the spelling bee. She smiled and stood up.

Now there was a softer conversation from up front. "What can we do? This is their country," her mother said, "But we can't give up."

"No, we can't give up," Apba responded in a calm, fierce voice, "don't worry. I'll never give up, even if it is their country."

"No, Apba, this is not their country. They might think so, but they're wrong. It's our country too," Stella whispered. If only she could make everyone understand that, if only she could act on what she believed in her heart.

She was startled by a slam. Stella walked to the front and saw her father walking away across the parking lot in the cold air, without his coat.

❦

"Go to sleep, Sung Ok," said her mother from the couch. She was turning the pages of a novel, but Stella could see that her mother wasn't concentrating. She kept looking up from the pages and staring at an empty space on the wall.

"No, Mama, I want to see if Apba's okay."

"It's midnight, and we have to go to church tomorrow." Stella looked over at her with pleading eyes.

"Go to bed." It was that same tone again.

As soon as she was in her room changing, the front door creaked. Stella ran to the top of the stairs to greet her father, but shrank back from what she saw. He looked like he had been in a fight. His shirt was soiled, his cheek was swollen, and his hair was disheveled. He swayed a little when his wife gave him some tea, and he crumpled onto the couch. He seemed confused. Like she had on that other night, Stella watched.

Then Mrs. Kim began speaking to him. She reminded him about their poor beginnings in the United States and how he had worked double shifts until he won his engineering job. She reminded him about how they had sacrificed to buy their own business and to learn English. Stella realized that she had never thought about how difficult it must be to learn English as an adult.

Her mother pretended not to notice Apba's appearance, his drunkenness. Then she talked about their achievements. She reminded him about how proud he had felt to have his children born in this country, and how well Stella was doing in school. She pointed out that Frankie, with his loud personality, could be much more accepted in the United States, and that Stella could marry well here, even though her parents came from humble families. She also mentioned how lovely and spacious their home was, which was possible only in this country. They had lived in an apartment in Seoul. Finally, she reminded him of two important points.

"You are encouraged to stand up for your rights in this country," she said, and Stella saw her father's arms drop in surprise. Her mother never spoke like this. "There are laws to protect Bong Kyu." She said something that really surprised Stella. "I am surprised," her mother continued, "that you can fight Mr. Jones to defend us in the store, but that you won't fight the soccer league manager to defend your friend." Mother discreetly picked up her father's cup and left the room. Stella was proud of her mother, but unsure of what would happen next.

Stella's father sat in the living room for a moment. The alcohol seemed to have left him while he listened to his wife. He looked toward the kitchen, where his wife continued in her place at the sink, washing dishes that were already clean. He walked over to the table by the stairs and picked up the phone. Stella stepped back a little from her place by the railing and looked at her watch. It was 12:30.

"Okay, I said do it. File the suit," Stella realized that he was talking to Mr. Kwon, the young lawyer who had also been at the stadium that night.

"I know it won't be easy."

"I agree to testify."

"I know it may take me away from work."

Apba listened to Mr. Kwon for a while before he spoke again. Finally, he said, "File the suit," and hung up the phone. A little while later, Mrs. Kim came back into the room with some dried squid for her husband to eat.

As her parents began to discuss the decision Mr. Kim had just made, Stella tiptoed back to her room. Apba was going to go to court. She felt a thrill. Apba would stand up for himself and for his friend. She thought for a moment, and then nodded to herself before stepping softly back into her bed.

Chapter 12

Diversity Requirement, Part I

In Language Arts class on Tuesday, the topic was diversity. At least, that is what Mrs. Murphy had written in big block letters on the chalkboard. Stella couldn't believe it, because all Mrs. Murphy ever talked about was grammar. All the teachers were doing something on that topic, it seemed. Good, thought Stella. Maybe now we don't all have to be pioneers.

"There are many different peoples in this great land," Mrs. Murphy began the moment the bell stopped ringing, "and they all contribute . . . something to the literature."

Maybe we'll read some stories now, Stella hoped, sitting up a little in her seat. She thought about the rows of books in her bedroom. Maybe now I'll learn something about people whose lives are like mine.

". . . but because of the upcoming state tests, we have limited time to . . . indulge in this . . . profound subject . . ."

"So we'll study more grammar?" chirped Eileen from the front row. Today, all the popular girls wore red together. In her thin blonde hair was a thick red headband, almost the same color as Mrs. Murphy's lipstick. In comparison, Stella's hair was incredibly thick and lush.

"Yes, dear," smiled Mrs. Murphy at her favorite student, "after we take a slight detour to fulfill this requirement." The teacher walked over toward her desk and turned to look at the class, seeming to focus on Stella, Marcus, and Rachel. Stella shifted uncomfortably in her chair. Why doesn't she just get on with it? Then Mrs. Murphy's gaze rested on Stella.

"So, Stella," Mrs. Murphy continued . . . Stella sat up, rigid. She hadn't finished all of her homework because she had been studying for the spelling bee . . . "instead of sampling all of that, shall we say, colorful literature, we'll simply have a discussion to sensitize ourselves." She looked at the thin gold watch on her fleshy pale arm.

"So, Stella, my dear," the teacher smiled as she walked over and put her hand on Stella's shoulder, "how does it feel to be an Oriental in this diverse society?"

All of the heads in the classroom seemed to turn toward her in one motion. She felt exposed, in the spotlight, like a freak. Stella had never felt more conscious of her dark hair and eyes, and smooth soft face, than she had at this moment. Her stomach twisted in agony. Her face blushed a deep red. Sitting motionless under the teacher's heavy, soft hand, Stella wondered how Mrs. Murphy could do this to her. There was nothing for her to say, so she was silent. Doggedly, frustratingly silent.

"Well, Miss Kim?" Stella bit her lip and looked at her hands, wishing for the first time in her life that she could jump up and punch the teacher. She was frozen. She was shocked.

"Well, I say, Miss Kim, you are surprisingly inarticulate today," said Mrs. Murphy, finally lifting her hand and turning toward the other students. "Any others? Any insights?"

"Well, Mrs. Murphy," said Rachel, sitting up in her chair, "it feels like you're twelve years old, you're a girl, and you hate being embarrassed. That's what it feels like to me, anyway, and I'm Jewish. Is that good enough?" Rachel pushed back her desk in disgust, staring angrily at the teacher. Mrs. Murphy stepped back a bit in surprise, her red mouth rounded a bit in an "O," and turned her back and walked back to her desk.

"Well, I think we've had enough of sensitizing for today, young people," she said, pulling out her top drawer. "Now if you'll just open your grammar books to page 263. . ."

Stella took out her book, upside down, and left it closed on her desk. Her gaze rested on Rachel, who rolled her eyes and grinned at her friend. "What an idiot," mouthed Rachel, so that no one else could hear.

For once, Stella didn't care if anyone else could hear. She was shaking, so furious that she couldn't think clearly. All she knew was that she would get even. She would show Mrs. Murphy . . . her ability, her intelligence, her ability to fit right in. She walked up to her desk and said, "I want an application for the spelling bee. I'm going to compete." Mrs. Murphy looked at her in surprise and handed one over.

Chapter 13

Standing Up

The next day was still depressing. They were serving Sloppy Joes again — twice in less than three weeks — but even though they soured her breath and thudded in Stella's stomach, she was too hungry to pass them up today. She walked past Ms. Queen to the food line.

Outside, the weather was still cold and wet. The chill crept easily under the thin blue fabric of her shirt — the wrong choice for the weather, but, she hoped, the right choice for fashion.

As she approached the food line, Rachel waved at her. Stella brightened until she saw Eileen. Despite herself, Stella's heart leapt with an irrational yearning to be like Eileen, to be with her. Stella felt some nails digging into her forearm and there stood her friend, just inches away from Stella's face. It seemed as if her wish were going to be granted.

A broad, toothy smile was pasted on her face, but her eyes weren't smiling at all. "Stella!" She paused. "Stella Kim," Eileen said, theatrically, looking at her friends for approval. "Why don't you sit with us?" Although Stella was hungry for food, she was hungrier still for acceptance, so she silently followed Eileen to the table. As if by prearrangement, Amanda, Heather, and Bobbi left together to get their lunch.

"I'll get your food, Stella. After all," she continued, bony hand resting again on Stella's arm, "you are coaching me in the spelling bee. It's the least I could do."

"No, that's okay."

"No, Stella, I insist," Eileen's eyes gleamed. Stella looked hungrily at the other students' full orange trays, but her dignity would not let her accept a free lunch from Eileen.

"A carton of milk is okay," she said finally.

Eileen walked off with her friends to get it. From her seat, Stella watched the other students. Rachel sat at the next table with Jesse and Marcus. They seemed to be looking at Stella as they talked. She smiled at them, hesitatingly, but they didn't seem to notice. Part of her wished she were sitting with them, talking about something interesting.

Stella sat alone for what seemed like a long time. When she looked up to see where Eileen and her friends were, they were all talking together and whispering by the check-out counter, but they stopped when they noticed Stella looking at them.

They giggled and waved at her, looked at one another and all came to sit down.

"Well, I have some news," said Eileen, as she handed the milk carton to Stella.

"Um, thanks," Stella picked up the milk awkwardly. "I guess."

"I overheard my parents talking. My father is taking on a new case," Eileen announced as she pulled open her bag of nacho chips. The smell of Sloppy Joes wafted over toward her from Rachel's table. Stella looked toward it.

"Oh, and what case is that?" asked Amanda.

"A Korean case," said Eileen, averting her gaze from Stella. Eileen pushed three chips into her mouth at once. Stella almost dropped her milk. This was not a friendly meeting.

"A Korean case?" asked Amanda, as if rehearsed, "what kind of case is that?" she said, and Stella noticed that no one at the table would look at her.

"This man my father knows," Eileen said, looking around the table significantly, "owns a stadium and runs soccer leagues. An indoor soccer stadium. And some Korean thugs are suing him. Can you imagine?" Eileen sat back and licked the cheese-flavored powder from her long bony fingers.

"Obviously, these Korean . . . men . . . are doing one of two things. They are either, trying to get money — my dad calls that extortion — or else they're trying to blame somebody else for losing some stupid game." Eileen finished licking her fingers and looked around at her captive audience. "Money or blame." "Money or blame," she repeated. "Well," Eileen continued, "it doesn't matter anyway, because they're going to lose and be forced to pay fines and maybe go to jail. But the funny thing is," Eileen continued, looking all the way around the table and stopping just before her gaze fell on Stella, "this one man's name is Kim. He's supposed to testify, along with a man who got arrested for trying to beat up the stadium owner. Some Bum Gook Chang or something. Move to America, try to steal your fair share, that's what my father says," concluded Eileen, still refusing to look at Stella.

By now, Stella's insides were like ice. She knew exactly what Eileen was talking about, and now everyone would know. Mr. Kwon was going up against Eileen's father in court. Stella felt sure that Eileen would always hate her because Stella's father had filed this suit. Her feelings changed swiftly.

She felt angry that her mother had made him do it, that they couldn't have just gone along. If she fit in, nobody would pick on her this much. Then she felt a bit of hope; maybe it wasn't too late to pretend it was someone else. For some reason, Stella glanced up toward where Rachel was sitting. Rachel leaned backward in her seat; Stella could swear that Rachel was listening. For some reason, Stella stifled the denial that was about to spring from her mouth. Then it got worse.

"Kim," said Eileen, reaching into the small aluminum bag for the last crumbs of nacho dust. She finally turned to her right and looked full into Stella's eyes. "That's your name, isn't it, Stella?" The table was silent. All the popular girls finally looked at her. She felt like an animal in a cage. Then Stella heard the whispering.

"Stella."

"Kim."

It sounded like two people. Stella looked from Amanda to Heather, both of whom covered their mouths with their fists and looked away. She looked at Eileen, who looked Stella right in the eyes and showed her teeth. "Is something the matter, Stella . . . Kim?" She smiled and cocked her head to one side. "Is something the matter, Stella . . . Kim?"

Stella heard it again.

"Stella."

"Kim."

"Stella."

"Kim."

Most of the girls at the table had their mouths covered now, and looked away from Stella. Some tried not to laugh. At the next table, Rachel was leaning backwards even more and had stopped talking with Jesse and Marcus. Jesse was building a tower of empty milk cartons while Marcus studied.

"Stella."

"Kim."

Stella gulped for air and willed herself not to cry. Just when she thought that she couldn't stand anymore, Eileen laughed and laid her hand softly on Stella's arm. She leaned over conspiratorially so that Stella could see the jagged ends of her small white teeth.

"But you're not like that, are you Stella?"

"You're not unsatisfied. Foreign. A poor sport." Stella knew that Eileen was talking about Stella's father. She was stunned, silent. Her stomach was rioting in distress. She felt ready to run out, feeling sick and crying, but her pride didn't let her. Or maybe she was just frozen still. Strangely, she remembered the time that Bronko and his friends had mocked her. She looked at Rachel.

"Besides," said Eileen, not stopping long enough for Stella to collect herself or even get help, "this Kim person is a dry-cleaner. Imagine that, my mother said, a dry-cleaner. A Korean dry-cleaner named Kim. Imagine that. He probably doesn't know enough English to testify. That's what my mother says. How funny." Eileen took her hand off Stella's arm and leaned back, looking at the circle of popular girls.

Stella was sure that everyone would see if she cried. Rachel was over there; these girls hated her. She glanced up at the clock over the double doors. If only the bell would ring . . .

"Stella's not a complaining foreigner, cry-baby, poor sport,"

Eileen repeated, nodding a signal at Amanda and Heather. They flashed fake smiles at Stella, who wished desperately that they were sincere.

"Are you, Stella Kim. Stella. Kim."

"That couldn't be you, could it, Stella. Because . . ." and now Eileen looked right into Stella's eyes again and this time, she didn't smile, "your dad's an engineer, isn't he?"

"And your mother . . ." now Eileen really zeroed in on Stella, "is a nurse?" Stella heard the echo of the words she had practically yelled at Eileen that day at her friend's house, just before Stella had left and refused to help Eileen study. Now she realized that she was being punished for not helping Eileen to prepare for the spelling bee.

"Does that mean she works as a nurse? Does your mother have a JOB as a nurse, Stella?" All the girls looked at Stella, with hostile, narrowed eyes and smug smiles, waiting for a response. Stella's eyes blinked back anger and fear. When she was just ready to cry in total desperation, she glanced up and saw Rachel, whose jaw was set. Obviously, Rachel was furious at Eileen, as she had been at Bronko that day, but this time, her friend remained silent. For some reason, Rachel at this moment reminded Stella of her Grandmother. Stella took a deep breath and looked at the circle of girls.

"It's none of your stupid business, Eileen," she said, jerking her arm away from Eileen, her so-called best friend. Stella stared through teary eyes at all the girls in blue, for the first time it seemed, right in the eyes. Her chin stuck out and she said, "Leave me alone!"

Stella pushed her tray away, with its unfinished milk. Just as Rachel said, Eileen was a user. Stella stood up and turned around.

"You can study for the spelling bee by yourself! You can't even do your own work! You're a creep! You're just mean!"

Stella couldn't believe what she had just said. She realized that she had just lost everything. She felt her hands shaking at the ends of her arms, as if they belonged to someone else. As she stood there, looking at the girls with their eyes opened wide in shock, the shaking increased, and she felt that she couldn't control herself any longer. She walked to the water fountain.

Then Eileen yelled back, "Oh, yeah! I can easily win! I'm a winner, just like my dad! Just like my mom. Like you know English, Stella. Like you can really beat me at English!"

Stella's legs felt numb, stiff, as she willed herself to walk forward past the tables of noisy students, she felt dozens of eyes glued to her. She felt her thick hair bounce against her shoulder blades and then fall around her face in a blessed shade as she took a shallow breath and leaned over the cool, sweating fountain to drink.

Small sips of icy water strung through her until the bell rang, and Stella was jostled out of the cafeteria with a stream of busy students. She expected to be hated, confused and lonely forever.

Stella knew, as she made her way to her next class, that she didn't have any friends anymore, but . . . then she noticed that her stomach didn't hurt. At the same time, embarrassment burned her face, and her fists clenched as she walked past Amanda. Stella glared at her, and Amanda stepped back. She had crossed the line, and there was no going back. The anger hit her in a wave; it felt strangely exhilarating.

❦

After school, Stella walked to the store for the first time, alone, through the cold spring air and across busy suburban roads. She felt reckless with anger. She didn't care if her Grandmother did yell at her, she just had to see her mom and dad.

She pulled open the door of the store. Her mother's eyes widened in surprise, but she quickly recovered herself. Stella's mother finished helping Mrs. Ontkean, who was picking up some alterations that she had waited so long to pick up because of Mrs. Kim's arthritis.

"See you tomorrow," Mrs. Kim smiled to her friend and then turned to her daughter. Stella stood under her mother's gaze and suddenly felt foolish, as if she were just a child who should go home. Then she surprised herself. She walked behind the counter, threw down her backpack, and started sorting clothes. Stella had the strangest thought that she was becoming like her Grandmother. Her mother shook her head.

Now she was free to work. When her father emerged, sweaty and tired, he looked at Stella. She paused in her work, afraid that he would yell at her. She was pleased when he said nothing. Then he broke into a big grin and walked away.

Time passed, and it got darker. Stella started to feel hungry and tired. She hadn't eaten anything for lunch, after all. She didn't know how she would get her work done tonight. She saw things differently in the late afternoon light. Her mother's wrist was wrapped in a tired-looking Ace bandage, which she had never seen before. The work in this store was grueling, even for two people. How would her mother manage by herself while father testified?

In the dark, Stella hadn't noticed the black Volvo pulling into the parking lot. It was the Engleharts' car. The license plates said, "WNNR," because Eileen said, her father was always a winner in court. The door opened. Every muscle in Stella's body was tensed to flee.

She felt her parents' presence behind her like a force holding her up. She realized that Mrs. Englehart would now know everything: that they were enemies in court, that her parents were only dry-cleaners, that she was a liar. Of course, she would tell Eileen, and Eileen would tell everyone, and everyone at school would hate her. She was glad she was close to her parents, and close to Rachel, because that would be all she had left.

Under the harsh fluorescent light, Stella noticed delicate wrinkles around her mother's eyes. Stella turned around and noticed her proud father working nearby. She stood firmly rooted at the counter. Something in her feet wouldn't let her leave; it was time to stand with her family. Through the darkness, it was hard to see Mrs. Englehart, but she stood, ready to face Eileen's mother.

When the door opened, Stella nearly giggled with relief. It was Rose, the Engleharts' maid. She stopped, looked at Stella with surprise and smiled warmly at the girl. Before coming to the counter or greeting Stella, she looked around and noticed Mrs. Kim, sitting at the old sewing machine in the front, rubbing her hands. Rose noticed the proud father standing behind his daughter in the back, shirt stained with sweat from the smelly, oppressive work with the machines. Rose paused and nodded to herself in silent understanding.

"Stella, your last name is Kim, isn't it, darlin'?" Rose asked.

"Yes, ma'am, it is," Stella responded, too shy to look up. She felt conscious for the first time that she didn't even know this middle-aged mother's last name. Stella had always known her just as Rose, the Engleharts' black maid from the city.

"God bless you, child," Rose said, laying a hand over Stella's.

Her parents stopped their work and watched.

Rose sighed and slowly lifted the torn evening dresses up onto the counter.

These were the clothes she and Eileen had played with that day after school. It felt like a lifetime ago. Rose paused again before she spoke.

"Now," Rose said, looking at Stella — "I hope you can let me leave these here past your 30-day limit. The Engleharts are going on vacation, and I won't be here to pick these up. I hope it's not too much of an inconvenience."

Stella knew this was a lie, because Eileen always bragged about her parents' trips and she had said nothing about a vacation. Stella's mother was finishing her last alteration in the pile, and Stella would put these in the back until mother's hands had a chance to recover. Stella and her Grandmother could do the simple alteration work for a few weeks until the Engleharts' special work was due.

"I'll see you, Stella," said Rose, nodding at Stella's parents on her way out.

"Thank you, ma'am," said Stella, so softly that she wondered if Rose even heard her.

Stella looked down and determined to find out Rose's last name, so she could address her the right way from now on.

Stella's mother looked at her carefully. Her father, after a moment, told her to count the money in the drawer and help her mother. They worked together another hour until closing. Then, as a family, they all went home to eat. Stella would be up late. The spelling bee and the court case were now less than a week away.

Be Who You Are

Stella sat cross-legged at the small lacquered table, rubbing her eyes with her wrists. Already, it was Thursday. The spelling bee would be Monday. Her head ached. It seemed impossible to master the advanced words in less than four days.

She looked longingly at the mementos of her friendship with Eileen. Her stomach twisted. Into her mind flashed images of last year's party with all the popular kids. Amanda and Heather were there. Jesse had been invited, but he didn't go. Marcus and Rachel had never been invited to Eileen's house. She bit her nails nervously, but then pushed the troubling thoughts away.

Her soft eyes lingered on the picture of Great America. Stella gnawed on the nails on her right hand. Eileen probably didn't mean what she had done Tuesday, she thought, mechanically.

Looking around her warm white room for some distraction,

she noticed the small plastic clock on her bedtable. It was ten p.m. As if to convince herself that it was too hard, she reached for the word list, focusing on the advanced words she hadn't yet studied: intolerant, cameraderie, stereotype. She flipped the cover closed and tossed the book onto the table.

As if by magic, the bedroom door slid open and the smell of smoke wafted into the room. In surprise, Stella's hands jerked back, as if she were guilty of something. From the doorway, Grandmother studied Stella.

Stella braced herself. Grandmother would call her lazy and make her work more. Although she looked down submissively, anger churned in her heart. She was old enough to make her own decisions about what was important.

Instead, Grandmother touched Stella gently on the arm and sat down on the bed. Stella, after looking carefully at Grandmother, sat down next to her. Without looking up, the old lady began to speak.

"I was born the second daughter of a scholar. Because the family had only girls, we were shamed. Because my father was a scholar, we were poor. This was when there was one Korea, not North and South as you think of it today. For women, there was no education past what you think of as high school. My sister and I were to be married, to produce sons to honor our husbands and families. It was my goal to be a good wife and mother."

Stella felt a little disoriented; Grandmother had never spoken to her like this before, and the look in her eyes was surprisingly gentle. Stella felt closer to her Grandmother, but at the same time she thought about how much she hated having to serve her stupid brothers. She tried to concentrate. This story seemed different.

"Because we were poor, we could afford no expensive presents, and I married a poor man. Your grandfather was a scholar, however, respected by his family as the keeper of the family records." Her wrinkled eyelids lowered for just a moment.

"Your grandfather wore traditional hanbok as he performed his honorable duty, illustrating and recording our family's history in beautiful Chinese calligraphy. It is an art form, as you will see when you next visit Korea." Stella's mind flashed from the Historical Society to the two stark paintings, which resembled letter-pictures, in their living room. "As he worked over his desk, I performed my duties. I swept our one-room home, folded the futons, pickled and buried our kim chee in the ground. I cooked for my husband's parents, fed bowls of rice to beggars, and honored our ancestors. It was my duty."

The old lady's shoulders raised a bit with pride. Stella struggled to understand her Grandmother's world.

"But we had no children," Grandmother continued, "it was a great shame. So I prayed for the gift of life."

Stella thought about how Grandmother spoiled her brothers. Her Grandmother treated her so differently. She felt as if her Grandmother were as hard on her as the old lady was on herself.

"Five years later we were granted a child. I ate extra beef to strengthen our son, and my husband chose his name."

Stella didn't know that her mother had a brother. She felt shocked and anxious about this missing family member. A memory came to her — Grandmother hiding her tears the day that Stella had said she never had a son. She felt a spear in her heart, somehow knowing the end of the story.

"A few years later, your mother came. When the children were becoming old enough to become their father's friends, the war broke out." This phrase confused Stella. It seemed to her that she still wasn't old enough to be her father's friend. The old lady continued, "The Communists wanted to take over our country, and brother fought against brother. Seoul was bombed, schools were closed, rice was scarce. It was chaos. There was murder. It was war. We saw bodies on the streets, and I could not shield my children from these sights. I tried only to protect . . ."

Here, Grandmother covered her mouth as if to cough, yet no sound came out. Stella sat on the edge of the bed, watching her every movement.

"Yet my husband clung to his artwork, out of respect to his

---

family, and out of defiance toward the war. Of course, there was no money now to support him. The children's clothes soon became ragged, and there was no more rice for beggars. We were close to becoming beggars ourselves."

"Then one day, the children and I returned from my husband's parents' home. A bomb went off. I grabbed my children's hands and we ran away from the fire and the dust. It would be safe in the alley, I was sure. So we ran away."

"I was sure we would be safe." Grandmother shook her head. "I was sure." She paused and covered her mouth again. Stella leaned toward her Grandmother and her damp eyes. She felt afraid, yet she yearned to hear the rest of the story.

"In the alley, my son was killed. I don't even know how. All I remember is that a bomb went off in the alley, and then my son was laying on the ground, limp," Grandmother paused, "I thought we were running away from the bombing, but we must have run into it. When I saw your uncle, I knew that he had been killed. I felt . . ."

Here, Stella's Grandmother clenched her fist, as if willing herself not to feel. She pressed her lips together and went on.

"When your grandfather learned of this he renounced his artwork and joined the fight. He printed flyers in the new simple and clear Korean alphabet, so that farmers and peasants could join the fight against the Communists. As with his scholarship, his war efforts were outstanding and gained him great esteem. He became famous. I feared for his life."

This was too much for Stella. Waves of horror, sadness and guilt washed through her. Her head swirled in astonishment at the brutality. She ached for her lost uncle and for her Grandmother's pain, some of which she had caused inadvertently. A dull, thudding resentment throbbed in her heart, because she had never been told of this before. Such chaos was impossible, yet it was true.

"Your grandfather was taken. We had remained in our same home, and finding his press was easy for the Communists. They waited until your mother and I went to his parents' house. They came and arrested your grandfather. When your mother and I came back home, the neighbors told us that the Communists had taken him. We never saw him or heard of him again . . ."

Stella's head whirled at the possibility that her grandfather might still be alive in North Korea. She wondered how her Grandmother had been able to survive for forty years with the uncertainty. She sat up with hope, thinking that they could work together to find him. When she looked at her Grandmother, something glinted in her small damp eyes.

"We survived the war, of course, but I was unprepared to work. We were very poor. Your mother and I had to live on the charity of relatives after my parents died. It was a shameful thing to be a widow and an orphan in Korea, and it was more shameful to be poor. I feared that my early sadness would become your mother's life. She had no power, no hope. It was not honorable to be so weak. So I educated your mother to be a nurse."

Grandmother's eyes glinted even harder, now. Stella thought that she was angry. Stella felt angry now, too.

"In Korea, you know, such work is shameful. For a young woman to work and to be exposed . . . to men, was shameful. She could no longer marry so freely as I had, but at least she had a profession. We lost even more status, of course. I despaired of finding her a husband. I had given up hope of finding mine again."

"Then my mother's sister suggested matchmaking. This man was from a poor and uneducated family. This was difficult for me, because our chief honor had been our education. Yet he had risen through the ranks in the war and was now studying to be an engineer. He had strength."

"So I met your father. Where your mother is soft, he is hard. Where she is dreaming, he makes plans. Your mother is her father's child, a scholarly dreamer forced into a practical life. I felt she would fail without a rudder. Your father is a plain man, but he is a rock. A family would not fail under his leadership."

Thinking of her strong Apba and her sweet soft mother, something bothered Stella. The memory of her parents' conversations downstairs came back, and she realized that she knew something about her mother that Grandmother didn't even know.

"Of course, we left Korea. A nurse with no father and a man with no name had no hope in that society. They decided to put their hopes into the next generation."

Stella sat up straighter. Grandmother seemed to be talking about her, now. She looked hopefully at the old woman. Maybe she would say something about how well Stella was doing and what a good daughter she was.

"They are successful now. In this community, parents do not mean as much, even among the Koreans. All work is honorable in this country. Your parents' business, although it is humble, makes all that we have possible. So we are in a new land, and there is hope."

Grandmother turned to look directly at Stella, her wet eyes glinting and strong. She covered Stella's hand with her smaller, wrinkled one. Stella felt a thrill, waiting for a rare compliment.

"Your parents' time has passed. Their choices have been made. Our family's only honor is in survival and the accomplishments of you children."

Grandmother lifted her hand from Stella's and smoothed the bedspread. There were so many disappointments in this old woman's life. Maybe that was why she was so demanding of Stella. Despite her understanding, Stella's hand felt cold, and she yearned for her Grandmother to cover and protect her like a child again. Slowly, though, she was realizing that this was impossible for Grandmother, and for herself, too.

"Frankie is powerful like your father, but he is all action and force and he needs someone wise to whisper in his ear." Stella thought of her mother, whispering to her father in the shop. Her Grandmother looked at her expectantly. Stella wondered if Grandmother expected her to whisper to Frankie. Stella felt like beating him, not whispering to him. She felt confused.

"Albert is soft. He is sensitive, like your mother. Yet, he is also fearful, as she is. He crumbles. He would not survive a war. I do not yet perceive his path. Your father will lead him well, I hope."

Stella felt desperate to know her Grandmother's thoughts about her. She needed to know that someone approved of her.

"Sung Ok," Grandmother said softly, looking at her. "Your parents' hopes for themselves are forgotten. They do not ask their own dreams for you." Grandmother paused and frowned a little. "In this country, I cannot ask my dreams for you," she said, "but I will tell you to be who you are, even though you are a girl." The familiar pain of inferiority stabbed at Stella once again, but she still waited. "Honor your history. That is enough. I have nothing to give you; all I can give you is where you are from. That is who you are. It is who I am as well."

Before Stella could respond, the old lady was gone. She had not scolded her or demanded that Stella study more.

Grandmother left the room just the way she came in — quietly, yet touching everything with her power.

Stella shook her head, not noticing that it was after eleven. She slid down off her bed and opened her spelling book. She began studying unconsciously, fiercely, not even knowing why.

At eleven-thirty, after Frankie and Grandmother had gone to bed, Albert came to Stella's room to say goodnight. He stared awkwardly at her open books and tired eyes. Stella understood that Albert was trying to grow up and decided to try to show him how. "Would you help me study?" she asked.

"Sure!" Albert replied, dropping onto the carpet as if he thought she'd never ask. "Let me quiz you!" He looked over the words before choosing one. He struggled to pronounce, "Idiosyncratically."

Stella smiled before she spelled it. She was correct. Albert grinned a little, impressed with his sister. "Certitude," he said next. She knew it. They studied for another half hour.

"Albert, you should go to bed," Stella said when he yawned for the third time. He shook his head. Nevertheless, she stood up to open her door, because it was so late. As she stood waiting for Albert to get up, she heard her father speaking on the phone. She motioned to Albert to stay still.

"Early in the week?" Apba said in Korean. "It will be difficult to leave the store. My wife is very busy." Stella paused, her hand on the doorknob. He was talking to Mr. Kwon. It sounded like Apba didn't want to testify. "Englehart's a political supporter of the judge? That's bad news." She shushed Albert, who was trying to ask her what was happening. If Apba didn't testify, then the case might not win.

"Okay," he continued. "We'll fight anyway. We're too far into this to back down now." Stella breathed a sigh of relief, at the same time realizing how difficult it would be. There was too much work at the store for one person. They would have to work late this week to make up for his absence, like Stella worked now to prepare for her competition. Their parents couldn't afford any stress at home this week.

"Albert, I have to tell you something." Stella turned to close the door. When she had finished explaining, she heard her father tell her mother that they would probably get the verdict in about a week.

Chapter 15

The Spelling Bee

Stella's stomach felt as if it were full of needles as she waited for math and the school day to end on Monday. It was April 22nd, the day of the spelling bee. All the seats in the auditorium would be filled. She looked from Rachel to Jesse to Eileen and her friends; none of them seemed nervous or worried.

"Miss Kim?"

Stella glanced at the clock. It was 2:50. Her mind flew to her parents' store, where her mother would be looking at the pile of Mrs. Englehart's alterations. It was too early in the day for her to make it to the competition.

"Miss Kim?"

Everyone else would be there. Mrs. Englehart would be there. All the popular girls would be there.

Mrs. Factor's hand tapped her desk. "Stella! Are you with us today?"

"I asked what the answer was to question thirty-seven."

"Oh, sure, okay," she rifled through her homework. It was uncharacteristically sloppy. She got the answer wrong, and Amanda laughed out loud. The sting in her red cheeks faded quickly as the clock's ticking reverberated in her mind.

The rough jangling scream of the bell startled Stella almost out of her seat. She barely heard Rachel saying, "You're the best! Don't be nervous!" Stella was the one taking the risks now; she was the one going on stage. Mrs. Murphy's announcement on the P.A. system didn't help either.

"Ladies and gentlemen, be sure to support your classmates and increase your knowledge by attending today's spelling bee . . ."

Stella pushed out of the door and into the hall, against the crush of students rushing toward the bus lines and home. She didn't even see the circle of admirers surrounding Eileen and Amanda, telling them they would win. It was time. The test was here.

❦

The stage lights illuminated the rows of empty folding chairs. No one was there. Stella stood by the front row of seats and wondered whether she had imagined hearing Mrs. Murphy's announcement. Two eighth-graders emerged from behind the heavy, blue velvet curtain carrying a long metal table with a piece of paper reading "JUDGES" taped to the front.

"OK, it's now." She drew in her breath, then noticed her armful of books. There was no time to return to her locker, but she couldn't afford to forget them. She walked up the five wooden steps at the edge of the stage, looking for a dark, empty corner. After arranging them neatly on the smooth wooden floor, Stella returned to the main area, which now swarmed with students hunting for their nametags on cold metal seats.

She walked stiffly to the third row. Jesse sat in the front, and Amanda sat in the row behind him. Stella tried not to be irritated by Amanda's blond hair as it whipped from side to side as she greeted all of her friends. Eileen was strangely quiet in the row behind Stella, but Stella couldn't turn around to greet her. She was afraid that something in her face would reveal too much to Eileen.

❦

From her place on the stage, Stella could see little. The faces in the audience, although not far away, looked like floating balloons. Peoples' features were blurry. Blinking back the spotlights' glare and blocking out the whispers and giggles of those around her, she looked again. If she craned her neck, she could begin to make out the features of those seated in the first row. She looked carefully at every seat. There was Mrs. Englehart. Next to her sat Jesse's mother, a chubby blonde woman. Stella's mother wasn't there. Stella drew her shoulders in and worked to convince herself that her mother's absence didn't matter, that she could do it on her own.

Mrs. Murphy walked out from the heavy velvet curtains into the spotlight. Her short, worn heels clicked on the shiny wooden floor. Her powder looked thicker beneath the glare. When she said, "ahem," the room quieted immediately.

"Ladies and gentlemen," she began, her red-lipped smile sparkling in the harsh light, "allow me to welcome you to the annual spelling bee."

The applause crackled, then roared. Stella realized that hundreds of people filled the seats. Her breathing accelerated as she thought about the price of this competition. The popular girls wanted her to lose, and when Amanda or Eileen won, she would have nothing. They would exclude her more than ever. She would be worse off than if she hadn't tried at all. The spotlights exposed her raw nerves.

"Please listen carefully as I explain the rules. . ."

Eileen leaned forward and whispered harshly, "My mother won this, you know! I can win it, too! And my father's a lawyer!" Stella sat fixed in her seat.

" . . . read the word aloud. The contestant then would be asked to spell it, although," she said, smiling again, "any boy or girl among these bright young people may ask for clarification, language origin, or an example sentence with the word."

"Furthermore," she continued, eyes shining as she looked

among the students and out toward the audience," the contestant may stop and start over, retracing the spelling from the beginning . . ."

This was the hard rule, Stella remembered.

" . . . but there can be no change of letters . . . "

Trying to push away thoughts of Eileen, Stella watched the audience file into their seats. There were Marcus' mother and father. She was Caucasian and short, a disc jockey downtown; he was Black and tall, a Biblical scholar. People never fit into your preconceived ideas, she thought, just as Rachel had said.

Mrs. Murphy turned to the students and asked, "Ready, contestants?" In the rows of metal folding chairs, some students grimaced and the others nodded. A soft murmur flowed through the audience. They became silent. The competition began.

At the front of the stage, Jesse leaned into the microphone. His thick straight hair fell across his cheek, and he had to push it back. No wonder Eileen thought he was cute, Stella thought, at the same time wondering why she was thinking about this. He blinked a little but didn't seem nervous. He must have studied this time. These first words would be easy, Stella nervously told herself, they would have to be.

"Laborious. Industrious, hardworking, diligent."

Stella picked at her fingernails, and snorted in derision. Jesse was definitely not laborious. Everything seemed so easy to him. He could break the rules all he wanted. Of course, he spelled it right.

"Essential. Necessary, indispensable." A fifth-grader misspelled it and stepped down the polished stairs. His empty seat gaped at Stella.

Toward the end of the round, Eileen stepped up to the microphone from the row where she had been waiting.

"Sanction," said Mrs. Murphy, pronouncing the word so deliberately with her bright red mouth.

"Is the origin sanctus, from the Latin?" She flashed a smile at her mother in the front row. Sure, her father must know Latin, thought Stella. He's a lawyer. Other students rolled their eyes.

Mrs. Murphy sanctioned Eileen, her pet, winning the spelling bee, thought Stella. Eileen spelled it correctly and flashed another toothy smile, this time at Stella, as she returned to her seat. Stella flinched.

Another girl now awaited her turn, crossing her legs and pulling at her hair as she leaned into the microphone. Stella stood behind the girl, with high shoulders and tense arms.

"I-N-T-O-L-E-R-A-N-T. Intolerant."

It was Stella's turn again. The microphone was too high for her. She couldn't see anything through the spotlights' hot, harsh glare.

"Excuse me, could you please repeat the word, please?" This was just like math class, where she had answered incorrectly.

"Disdain," the judges and audience watched her.

"D-I-S-D-A-I-N. Disdain."

Stella scurried back, not noticing that Eileen watched. Safe again in her seat, she followed Amanda's approach to the microphone. Amanda strutted. From the front row, her family cheered. Stella was surprised to learn that Amanda was smart; she never acted like it in school. Before Stella knew it, another round of beginning words had ended with no one dropping out.

"Now, contestants, we will proceed to the intermediate words."

Amanda was up again.

"G-A-U-K-I-N-E-S-S. Gawkiness."

"Incorrect."

Stella was as surprised at Amanda's mistake as she had been at her intelligence. She flipped back her long blond hair and her little brother booed the judges, as the audience applauded her effort.

After another turn, Stella could see a sixth-grade boy entertaining the audience. When he answered correctly, he raised his hands in exultation and then placed his fingers on his neck, as if taking a pulse. Stella wondered why anyone would want to draw extra attention to himself. She awaited her next turn. The rounds went faster now.

"P-R-O-W-E-S-S. Prowess," Stella spelled correctly. Hands in her pockets, she walked back to her seat. She wondered if her mother were there, but she was doing okay. She sat up straight in her chair and looked around. Jesse's mom had big blonde hair like an old Texas cheerleader, thought Stella, at least that's what Rachel said. She noticed Rachel sitting in the audience, and smiled at her friend.

The round passed quickly and Eileen was up again.

"I-N-D-U-B-I- . . ."

"Indubitable. . ." Eileen started again. She knew that she couldn't change the spelling.

"I-N-D-U-B-I-T-A-B-L-E." It was correct, and it was just like Eileen. Her mother sat rigid in her seat, clapping with stiff long fingers, watching her daughter like a hawk.

The third round was tense. The funny sixth-grade boy had been eliminated. A shy girl who hid behind her hair was gone, too. The remaining students moved up into the first three rows. The audience murmured. Eileen moved into a seat next to Stella.

She felt Eileen staring, but Stella focused her eyes straight ahead. It was too late to change anything. The people in the audience were quiet, and the lights continued to glare. Butterflies flew around Stella's stomach, and she struggled to keep her fingernails out of her mouth. She wished that Eileen would quit staring. She felt sure she was going to lose. The words were coming more quickly. It was Stella's turn again.

"Cameraderie," said Ms. Murphy.

"Cameraderie," said Ms. Murphy.

Was the root word camera? Was it comrade? C-O-M?

"Miss Kim?"

Oh, camerade-

Stella spelled it quickly and sat down.

"Stereotype." Jesse was at the microphone again, smiling behind his thick brown hair.

"Definition, please."

"A standardized mental picture held in common by members of a group and representing an oversimplified opinion."

Jesse spelled it properly, right away, and gave Stella a long, close look when he was finished. Stella wondered what he knew about stereotypes, and why he was staring at her.

At the end of the intermediate round, only Jesse, Stella and Eileen remained. The advanced words were the real contest, Stella thought. But she was worried, she should already have beaten Jesse.

"Certitude." Stella spelled it correctly and quickly, thinking of her Grandmother.

"Idiosyncratically," said Mrs. Murphy. Again, Jesse asked for a definition. Stella looked at him out of the corner of her eye and realized that she didn't know much about him.

"In a manner peculiar to the individual, eccentrically." Once again, Jesse recited the spelling almost automatically. Stella saw him glance at her again. She wondered if it were some kind of a joke.

Eileen took another turn and sat down, and before Stella even knew it, it was her turn again. Stella spelled her next word, "nocive," carefully, remembering that nocive was overconfidence. Jesse and Eileen wouldn't allow her to be overconfident, that was for sure.

The next word was hibachi. That was easy, thought Stella. Eileen stood at the microphone, right hand fluttering over her straight blond hair. She rolled back on her heel, and gawked at the audience.

"Hibachi. H-I-B-O-" Stella quit listening, but in the background Eileen started again.

"H-I-B-A-" Stella wondered what her next word would be. She wished she had studied harder, and was afraid that Eileen would beat her.

The audience groaned. Stella looked up to see Eileen spinning on her heel with her hands raised at her chest, mouth hanging wide open. Stella's heart bunched up a little for her old friend, whose mother sat watching her every move with steely eyes. As Eileen walked to her seat, Mrs. Englehart's gray eyes fixed on Mrs. Murphy like a laser beam. The teacher didn't flinch.

The audience clapped. Looking out in the light, Stella could see more clearly. Eileen was already gone. . . she and Jesse were left. Stella realized that they were applauding for her.

The winner and the runner-up both appeared in the paper. Mrs. Murphy's desk photo would display Stella's face all next year. She smiled a little. Jesse would take her place if she couldn't compete in the regional contest, she thought, that is, if she could beat Jesse. Of course, she could. She only had to . . . She sat up straighter. Jesse was at the microphone again.

"Prejudicial. Tending to injure or impair: hurtful, damaging." Stella scowled at Jesse. He got all the easy words. He winked at her as he took his seat.

Her eyes adjusted to the lights, Stella noticed her mother in the third row. Her heart leapt in excitement and eagerness. She got up from her seat.

"Simultaneity." She spelled it correctly and sat in the empty seat in the front row, next to Jesse. Her turn came again.

"Immaleable. Unyielding, rigid." What was unyielding, she wondered, . . . time was running out . . . "Spell the word, please, Miss Kim," said Mrs. Murphy.

"E-M-M-A-L-A-B-L-E." A pause held the auditorium, then the audience groaned in one voice. The audience burst into applause. She realized that Jesse had won.

Stella shook Jesse's hand, as her father had taught her to do. She felt a strange jolt of electricity when their hands touched, but before she could think about what it was, she found herself surrounded by a swirling chaos of bodies and lights. She couldn't see over the crowd to find her mother and felt jostled and lost amid the shoulders and elbows of everyone who seemed to tower over her at this moment, more than at any other in her life.

She saw nothing clearly, heard only noises and felt utterly lost. She could only think dumbly, again and again, that she had left the group for this. Stella could see none of the popular girls in the chaos, only a glimpse of regal Mrs. Englehart in her tan tweed suit and pearls talking heatedly with Mrs. Murphy. Stella decided to give herself up to the scene. Her thoughts melted away, and in their place was left only a sense of longing, quite familiar, and a sense of emptiness, which was quite new. Without thinking, Stella realized with sudden and terrible clarity that she had no clear place now.

Just then, a light exploded nearby. She covered her face with her forearm before realizing that the photographer had taken her picture. Now, she thought, now it's done. A certain pride bloomed in her heart, despite her sense of isolation. At least she had gotten into the paper, she thought. At least she had beaten Amanda and Eileen, even if she didn't place first. She knew English better than Eileen did, it seemed, even if Eileen's father was a lawyer.

After the auditorium emptied out, Rachel came over, a warm smile softening her strong face. Her blue-green eyes twinkled with respect for her friend. "Congratulations!"

"Thanks for your help," Stella said softly, trying with all her seesaw. She saw the backs of Eileen, her mother, Amanda and Heather as they left the auditorium. She imagined Amanda telling Eileen that if Stella hadn't entered, then Eileen would have been second, and Eileen's picture would be in the paper, like her mother's had been. Stella imagined Eileen's mother being angry at her, too. Rachel waited patiently.

Stella struggled to understand her feelings. She pursed her lips together and looked at Rachel, who said, "I'll call you tonight. You probably want to see your mom." She smiled, "I knew you could do it, Stella."

Meanwhile, Jesse and his fleshy, blonde mother walked by. His white teeth gleamed as he smiled boldly at Stella. For the first time, she noticed his eyes sparkling. When Stella saw the winner's certificate in his hand, though, all she could think was that he would be the one to receive the trophy in an award ceremony tomorrow at school, instead of her.

The auditorium had emptied out. Stella's brain felt dull, as if it were padded with cotton. She felt she was forgetting something. As soon as she finished one thing, there was another, she thought. The social studies research paper was her next project, in fact she was behind on it already. It was due in two weeks, but in studying for the spelling bee, she had neglected it. She hoped that life would not always be so complicated.

Stella finally looked around for her mother and discovered

that she had stood behind her daughter while she spoke to Rachel. Stella wondered why her mother hadn't stepped in to say hello. Stella blushed a little when she turned her eyes toward her mother's gentle face.

Touching Stella's back lightly, her mother said, "That boy is smart." Stella nodded and looked down, embarrassed again, this time for herself. She felt it was a mistake to let her family know that she had studied for this. Her mother must think she was stupid, thought Stella. Looking up, she was surprised. Mother's soft, brown eyes, so much like Stella's, shone with warmth. Stella didn't understand why her mother complimented Jesse.

Mrs. Murphy approached Stella and her mother and said, "Congratulations, Stella! You did well to place second. I know you worked hard on this, but Jesse is a gifted child. You must be proud of your daughter, Mrs. Kim." Stella was confused. Jesse wasn't gifted; he was weird. Then Stella noticed Mrs. Murphy standing respectfully in front of them, awaiting Mrs. Kim's response. Something was different this year, Stella thought.

Stella's mother bowed, her soft "thank you" buried below her thick dark hair. Stella couldn't believe that her mother was acting so . . . Oriental. She wished that she would just shake hands, like Mrs. Englehart did. Suddenly, Mrs. Murphy was gone.

gone.

"Sung Ok, I'm leaving now." She could hardly hear her mother. "Study hard. Be home to help with dinner."

"Sure, Mom," Stella replied in English in case any of her friends heard. There weren't too many people left, though. In the commotion of people folding up chairs and clearing the stage, Stella's mother was gone.

After finishing a computer search on immigration in America, Stella grabbed her coat from the back of her chair and left the library. It had been a long, long day. She was relieved that no one else was at the library, because she didn't know where she fit anymore. She had closed the door on one life, she knew, and she couldn't see what awaited her through the next door. It was frightening.

Stella walked softly through the green-carpeted hallway and out through the library's front door. As she pushed it open, she noticed that the sky was still blue. The days were getting longer. Maybe the soccer team will be good this summer, she thought. Maybe she would go out for it. She laughed at herself, bitterly. Maybe she was the most popular girl in school. Maybe pigs can fly.

She walked slowly, by herself, studying the small green buds emerging on the branches of the trees. Stella was tired, and she concentrated on crossing each long square of concrete to propel herself, block by block, back home. Then, as the sky began turning red and she had finished her seventh block, she stopped and stood stock still, remembering. Her books. The image of a white math textbook and two spiral notebooks tucked in a dark, dusty corner of the auditorium appeared in her mind.

In her blue coat, her dark hair floating softly in the warming wind, Stella stood silently at the corner, two blocks from her house. She grimaced, and her eyes filled with tears. She knew that if she went back to school, then Grandmother would yell at her for being late. If she left her books at school, then she would be unprepared for math, disappoint Apba, and lose a homework grade. Resigned to failure either way, she took a step toward home.

❧

Stella Kim sat at her dining room table eating kim chee, surrounded by the warmth of her family. To her right sat her mother, lifting up steaming rice with her chopsticks. To her left sat her father, dipping rolled pancake into the soy sauce. Stella looked at her mother, home so early from a difficult business, with father, casually eating, providing no explanation.

Albert and Frankie sat across from Stella, heads bowed over their plates, flashing forks that plowed food into their mouths. Next to Stella sat Grandmother, who smiled slightly as she got up to refill Stella's plate. The gulp of the rice cooker closing woke Stella a bit, and she opened her mouth to ask why they were home. Just then, her mother and father's eyes locked together in an expression of satisfaction and pride. Stella exhaled slowly and reached for more rice. She had done well after all. She had done well.

Chapter 16

Diversity Requirement, Part II

In homeroom that Tuesday, Stella was talking to Rachel when she heard a commotion out in the hallway. The girls stopped talking and tilted their heads in the direction of the door. No one else seemed to hear it.

"Inappropriate curricular content!" was the phrase that she heard. The voice sounded familiar, but altered. It was rising, becoming more and more shrill.

"Newest and most updated spelling list, incorporating multicultural concepts," came Mrs. Murphy's voice. "Required by the state."

"Ill-conceived. Not appropriate for American children. Why should my daughter know how to spell Chinese words?" came the other voice, uncomfortably familiar to Stella. "Those . . . words are not fairly applied to American children. These are American children, you know! Not Chinese!" Stella squirmed in her seat. Now she was straining to listen. She shushed Rachel. Rachel shrugged.

"When I won this contest, before you were ever teaching at this school, Mrs. Murphy, there were no such ridiculous foreign phrases being used. I demand a review of the . . . booklet." The women in the hallway were silent for a moment.

"If you do not satisfy me, I will have to take this matter to a higher level!" came the voice again, nearly shrieking by now. The other students stopped talking. Some grinned. Everyone listened with interest, except Eileen. She paged through her notes, as if nothing were happening. The pages turned faster and faster.

The voices became clearer. Mrs. Murphy's voice was raised, too. "Mrs. Englehart," she said, and Eileen lowered her blond head even further, "Your daughter did not know how to spell the word. And besides, she violated a rule by spelling it differently the second time. You are familiar with those rules, Mrs. Englehart. She lost fairly. Third place isn't anything to be ashamed of!" Eileen had buried her head in her book.

The class was silent. Amanda and Heather were wide-eyed and aghast. They rolled their eyes and opened their mouths in disgust, but Eileen didn't respond. "I can't believe Mrs. Murphy," whispered Heather, loud enough for the class to hear.

The discussion continued. "This newfangled rule . . . having to use the same letters if one begins again . . . was not in place

160

formerly . . . isn't fair when contestants realize that they have made an error . . . " Mrs. Englehart fell quiet. Rachel caught Stella's eye, and Stella understood. Eileen didn't really care about the spelling bee. She had tried for her mother, who only wanted her picture in the paper. Stella looked at Eileen compassionately, but for once Eileen wasn't looking at anyone. Stella hoped for her sake that Mrs. Englehart would apologize.

"The principal will address this. She, at least, is professional," Mrs. Englehart concluded. Stella pretended she was interested in her textbook. While everyone stared at Eileen, Mrs. Murphy entered the room, shaking her head.

"Well, it seems that our spelling bee awards may be held up a few days," she said, wiping the hair back from her face and covering her hand with powder, "but allow me to congratulate the winners, Jesse and Stella, in places one and two. Your pictures will be published this week, and you will go to the regional spelling bee together in June."

All the students looked at them. Rachel stared at Stella with frank admiration. Stella sat self-consciously, and looked over her shoulder at Jesse, who seemed to be sleeping again.

"Well, stand up!" said Mrs. Murphy. "Stella, you should at least know how to acknowledge attention! Bow or something!" Stella just laughed. She didn't bow, Jesse remained asleep, but the class applauded.

The applause ended quickly, but the thrill remained in

Stella's heart. Eileen had pretended not to hear Mrs. Murphy, but everyone else had clapped. She felt solid. They noticed her, and this time, not for being different. For being good. Maybe she would find a place after all.

Homeroom was almost over. Stella leaned over and said, "Hey, Rachel. Why don't you come over today?"

Rachel smiled. "I'd love to," she said. Then Rachel smiled widely at Stella. "And I'll bring Jesse. He'd like to see you, too."

Chapter 17

The Newest Pioneers

On Thursday, they were discussing pioneers in social studies, in preparation for the research paper. Eileen was talking her head off. "My ancestors were pioneers. They were farmers. They lived in Iowa and then moved to Montana. Then my grandfather moved back here to work in the factories in Chicago. And now my daddy's a lawyer!" Stella rolled her eyes.

Jesse chimed in. "My family immigrated from England four hundred years ago, and they settled in Connecticut." Stella could hardly believe it. "Sure, Jesse," she said under her breath, but she grinned at him. She had had fun with him and Rachel on Tuesday. He had asked her about the Korean stuff in their house, and had even talked to Grandmother for a while.

"Do you want to speak up, Stella?" Ms. Queen asked with a smile.

"No, I don't know anything about pioneers." She felt like

everyone was staring at her.

Of course Koreans weren't pioneers, she thought. She wondered what kind of pioneers took a plane to Los Angeles in the 1980s and never set foot on a farm.

Ms. Queen showed the class a world map. She put a star on each country where a student had ancestors. She pointed to Ireland and England, and to Germany, where Eileen and Jesse said their families came from.

Then she asked other students where their families came from. Some were from Yugoslavia or the Soviet Union, before it turned into different countries. Some were from Iran. Someone else was from Chile. Stella sat up in her chair and watched closely. Someone else was from Canada.

"Wasn't anybody originally from America?" When no one answered, Ms. Queen said that there must not be any Native Americans present. "These peoples used to be called Indians, because Columbus thought he landed in India when he arrived here from Spain 500 years ago." That's goofy, Stella thought. People are so wrong about other people sometimes. Like with friends — she had been wrong to think that Eileen was her friend and that Rachel wasn't.

Finally, Ms. Queen pointed at Africa and Asia. "Aren't anyone's ancestors from here?" Marcus raised his hand.

"My family is from Africa a long time ago, but no one knows what part. Another part of my family is Irish, though. County

Cork."

"Ireland?" Stella mouthed to herself. She thought that Black people were only Black. Then she remembered seeing his parents at the spelling bee. She realized that she could be wrong about other people too.

"My family is from Korea," Stella said, finally, "but I was born here."

"South Korea?"

"Yes, Seoul. They lived through the Korean War." Jesse looked at Stella with interest.

"My grandfather fought in that war," said Marcus.

"Which side?" asked Stella.

"The American side, Stella," Marcus answered, sarcastically.

"No, which side of your family?" She felt a little embarrassed.

"Oh, my father's side. It was the first war where the troops were integrated. Before that, Black soldiers had to fight in all-Black units." The class listened respectfully. Ms. Queen put a star on the country, almost covering it. "It's small but mighty," Stella said softly.

"Do you know what you all are?" asked Ms. Queen at the end of the period.

Eileen giggled and said, "Students." Amanda and Heather cracked up.

Marcus raised his hand and said, "Pioneers?"

"Yes," said the teacher, silver earrings flashing in the bright spring light.

"How can we all be pioneers?" asked Stella. She thought that only people like Jesse and Eileen had the right history.

"Pioneers," Ms. Queen responded, "were – and are – people who left their homes and, with great courage, headed to America to make a new life for themselves and their children. Sometimes they came against their will — but what they have in common is that they sacrificed to come here.

"Some were English and settled in Eastern cities, some were farmers who moved to the Great Plains. Some, to our shame, came on slave ships and had to fight to become free. Others arrived on trains, from Mexico or Canada, and some flew on jets, from South Korea." The young teacher smiled at Stella.

"You mean we're pioneers too?" she thought aloud. Maybe she could do a paper on her own family's history. Maybe she would even write about kim chee. For the first time, she felt like she had something in common with all the other kids.

A Verdict

Spring finally arrived that Thursday afternoon. It was windy and bright. Soft new green grass was emerging from winter's dull brown turf, but it was still a little sharp, a little biting, in the air. In the backyard, Albert, Frankie, and Stella played soccer. At 5:30 Stella yelled, "Time to clean up!" As they were coming in, their parents' burgundy sedan pulled in the driveway. Stella was surprised. Their father jumped out of the car to kick the soccer ball with the boys. Curiously, Stella followed her mother inside.

"Set the dining room table, Sung Ok!" said Grandmother. Stella wondered why they were home. They had eaten dinner together last week. When Grandmother told her to set another place, Stella was even more curious. Her father and brothers came together through the door.

At six o'clock, the front door opened. Mr. Kwon, Apba's

lawyer, stood waiting in his blue pinstripe suit. "Welcome! Welcome!" said Grandmother, wiping her hands on the wet dishrag. "Take off your coat!" Mr. Kwon bowed before slipping off his shoes.

"Hello, Stella," Mr. Kwon said, turning toward the dining room where she stood. Most Korean adults didn't even know her American name. She didn't know why he was smiling.

"Good job on the spelling bee. Your parents are proud of you." He must have seen her picture in the newspaper. Mr. Kwon was being nice. Stella blushed.

Apba sat with Mr. Kwon while Stella prepared dinner with her mother and Grandmother. Albert and Frankie came down from the upstairs bathroom, where they had been washing up. Frankie had been unsuccessful. He still had a smudge of dirt on his upturned nose. Albert looked almost mature, Stella thought. The boys quietly walked past Mr. Kwon to the table and sat down. They didn't know how to speak to adults.

Soon, they were eating a formal Korean dinner, with broiled fish, kim chee, vegetable pancakes, and barbecued beef. Apba poured sake for Mr. Kwon, like an honored guest.

The rich pungent smells of the meal made Stella feel comfortable and secure until she looked around at the smiling adults and realized that something had happened. She was so absorbed in her thoughts that it was a moment before she realized the adults were talking.

"So Englehart was completely unprepared," said Mr. Kwon. Stella gawked at Mr. Kwon.

"We got an early court date, because it was in a suburban court. Englehart bluffed about knowing the judge. He didn't even know the materials," Mr. Kwon pushed back his empty plate and looked around the table. "It was almost too easy." Stella couldn't believe it; they had won the case, and Mr. Englehart had been disgraced. Stella wanted to leap out of her chair and yell.

"Then when they lost, and the stadium owner was ordered to pay damages to Bong Kyu and the Asians he had kicked out of the stadium, he was understandably mad at his attorney. The owner shouted at Englehart in court and almost received a contempt citation!"

Stella couldn't believe this. That man who had treated her father disrespectfully had to pay damages. She felt relieved for her Apba, whose life had been so difficult in the last few years. He must have felt terrible to have been insulted like that. There was justice. She sat still, but her spirits soared like the spring wind. She felt that things couldn't possibly get any better.

Mr. Kwon continued. "Then Englehart looked at me and said, if you can believe this, that it wasn't his fault! He didn't have time! This wasn't his specialty!" Wavy-haired Mr. Kwon threw back his head and laughed.

Mr. Kim slapped the table and burst out laughing. Stella's

mother covered her mouth to hide her laughter. Above her delicate hand, her soft eyes darted from Mr. Kwon to her husband. Then, she caught Stella's eye and together they smiled.

In the meantime, Albert and Frankie shoveled in the food in with their forks, unaware of the court case or of anything else, it seemed. Finally, Albert sensed Stella's stare and looked up, eyes lighting on all of his elders sharing a joke.

"This man blames someone else for losing! He has no pride at all!" said Mr. Kim, shaking his head of thick black hair. Stella was proud of him for taking the risk and fighting. Stella remembered trying on Mrs. Englehart's clothes that day. The family had seemed so perfect and strong.

"I don't think he expected me to be able to speak English, or something, so maybe he didn't prepare," said Mr. Kwon. "Oh, well," said the young attorney, picking up a last piece of beef with his chopsticks, "live and learn."

As she got up to help with the dishes, Stella smiled shyly at Mr. Kwon. She fumbled his plate, almost knocking over his sake glass. He picked it up and turned to Stella's father to continue talking.

The telephone rang. Her Grandmother grabbed Stella's arm and said, "That girl Eileen is lonely, Sung Ok. She is lonelier than you are."

"What are you . . .?" Stella hurried away with her next load of dishes so that she could get the call. Maybe it would be Rachel. "Oh, hi, Eileen," said Stella as she held the receiver. Stella looked at her Grandmother, who had a strange expression on her face. "No, I put away my math a while ago. We have company for dinner. What's up?" Stella spoke impatiently. The adults were suddenly quiet.

"Thank you." Eileen had congratulated her on second place, despite what Mrs. Englehart was doing. "A C.D. player? To make you feel better? But your birthday's next week!" Stella gasped. She had almost forgotten about the birthday party.

"Your birthday party? Next Saturday?"

Everyone would be there. An invitation meant that you were Eileen's friend. That still meant a lot. She thought about the popular girls leaving the auditorium together after the spelling bee. She thought about how alone she had felt. The adults sat silently.

"Yes, I'm here." She didn't know what to say. Her stomach hurt again. This was like giving Eileen the answers. But this time, Stella thought about how she felt before she agreed to do anything. She looked around and saw her mother watching her curiously. The men looked past their chopsticks and empty glasses. Her brothers squirmed in their chairs.

Stella noticed her Grandmother watching from the side of her eye in the kitchen. She covered the receiver with her hand as she remembered Grandmother's horrible story. Her

Grandmother was tough. She had a brief, painful thought about her grandfather. Then she looked at Mr. Kwon, who was a winner, like her parents. She finally took her hand off the receiver.

"Well, Eileen, I'd like to go but I'm busy on Saturday," She took a deep breath and continued, "helping my parents in their dry-cleaning store. . . . Yes, their dry-cleaning store. And then," she may as well put it all on the line, "then I had plans to get together with Rachel." She listened for a while and raised her eyebrow. Stella remembered her Grandmother's comment. Could Eileen be lonely?

". . . I could ask Rachel. If she wants to come, and you don't mind us coming late, I'd love to . . . Oh, I don't know what I'll wear tomorrow. Call me later. I'm sorry, we have company. I have to go."

Stella hung up the phone. She took a deep breath and looked at her Grandmother, whose back was turned. Stella felt sure that Grandmother had been watching her with that same light in her eyes that Stella saw whenever she stood up for herself in a fight, but there seemed to be more to it than that. Then, Stella breathed in again and noticed something remarkable. Her stomach didn't hurt, not at all.

For the first time, she felt all right after talking on the phone with Eileen. Maybe her body was trying to tell her something. Maybe she should stand up now, as Grandmother did, as her parents did, and help lead the family. Maybe she could fit in by being different, by being strong. Come to think of it, that's what Rachel and Jesse did. And Marcus. They never pretended to be anything they were not.

Maybe she had something to offer after all. Stella breathed out and her shoulders relaxed. When she breathed in again, the aroma of kim chee smelled strong and good. Her hand rested on the metal railing at the foot of the stairs. Her parents watched her. She felt like the center of attention again, just like in school. Then Stella surprised herself. She broke into a smile so big that the edges of her eyes crinkled.

꧁

After dinner was finished, Stella, her parents, and Mr. Kwon sat together in the living room. Albert had left to join Frankie downstairs, but Stella wanted to stay with the adults. They discussed the Korean community, social clubs, and church politics. She felt a part of their world for the first time. When the telephone rang, she took her time getting up to answer it.

"Jesse!" Her hands shook with excitement. She turned her back on the group in the living room.

"A . . . a movie!?!" Her voice was barely over a whisper.

"Um, um, we have company. Yeah, we have company now. Um, can I . . . can I call you back?" She almost dropped the phone on the stairs. When she sat down again with the adults, she squirmed in her seat. Her parents studied her face, which felt prickly with excitement. She wished she were in her room, or on the phone with Rachel, or even on the phone with Eileen. She didn't follow the rest of the conversation.

❦

Later that evening, after Mr. Kwon had left, her mother came into Stella's room and held out her hand. Stella stood up, curious, taking her mother's hand and following her out of the room. Her father was downstairs, watching the Bulls with her brothers. Grandmother had gone to bed. She wondered if her mother needed her help.

Stella followed her into her parents' crowded bedroom. On the dresser, besides a television and rows of framed family pictures, sat two jewelry boxes, one higher and closed with a dragon clasp, and one simple and low, with a red lacquered surface covered with flowers.

Her mother took this box and sat on the bed, motioning for Stella to sit next to her. As Stella joined her mother on the soft, down-covered bedspread, her mother removed the lid and looked at her daughter.

"When I went to nursing school, my mother said that I was becoming strong enough to help my family. It was a hard profession to learn in Korea but necessary for us to survive. I am glad I went, but it changed me. I became no longer soft. Changing is difficult," her mother said, looking into Stella's eyes, "but necessary. Girls must be strong now, like boys are, because everyone is responsible to lead. Your Grandmother will never admit that, but she knows it is true."

"Sung Ok," she said, opening up the fabric covering a small jewelry case inside the box, "you are growing strong now. You are young to fight, but you fight well. You are becoming a little like my father, I think." Her mother's eyes filled with tears. She swallowed hard and continued, "I am proud of you." Stella flushed with pride and joy, deeply surprised at these words by her mother, spoken to her for the first time ever. Her mother opened up a small jewel case and took out a necklace, a thick strand of woven gold, and fastened it around Stella's neck. "I consider you my helper now, to help and lead this family."

Stella felt a peace and excitement unlike anything she had ever known. She realized that her mother must have understood her conversation with Eileen, that she even knew who Eileen's father was. She probably understood who Rose was, too. And . . . Stella couldn't imagine what else her mother understood. Her mother stood up to put the lacquered box away.

"I hope you give this to your daughter when she becomes strong, too." She hugged her daughter. "Now go say goodnight to your father and brothers." Stella smiled at her mother through happy tears, unable to say anything at all, and proudly displayed her necklace over her pajamas as she walked downstairs.

As she leaned over to hug her father, he said, "Why are you wearing a necklace over your nightgown? Take it off when you go to bed!" She frowned a little. Her brothers didn't even look up when she said goodnight, but she turned around before going up the stairs. Stella caught her father watching her with a smile.

Chapter 19

You Know What To Do

That last Friday in April, the day before Eileen's party, Stella felt on top of the world as she walked home in the warm spring air. Despite Mrs. Englehart's complaints, Stella had received her second-place award in front of the whole school. Amanda was suddenly trying to gossip with Stella about Eileen, but Stella was sick of these popular girls' mean games. There were so many changes. Stella pulled open the door of her house, feeling very grown up.

Whap! A pillow hit her before she even made it inside. Whap! Another one got her before she saw where the first one was coming from. It was time to counterattack. Stella threw down her books and leaped over the couch, pursuing Frankie. If she could get him, then Albert would quit.

Frankie sprinted past the aquarium, jumped over the end table, and raced around the dining-room table. He allowed

Stella to get within inches and then barreled into the kitchen. Laughing but determined, Stella followed. This time, she would get him. Things would be different around here.

"Aiy!!!" yelled Grandmother, as Frankie knocked into her, spilling her bowlful of batter and wooden spoon onto the floor. "You criminals!" she yelled at the two. Stella halted. It would be different, all right, she thought as she tried to control her breathing. It would be worse. Blushing, Stella stooped down to scoop up the sticky mess.

"I'm sorry, Grandmother," she said, keeping her head down. Why can't . . . It's not . . . If only . . . Stella's thoughts started and stopped. Grandmother was dead silent. Stella awaited a reprimand, but strangely, she wanted to laugh as well. Suddenly, Grandmother gave her a shove.

Grandmother grinned and held out two ice cubes. A mischievous glint in her eyes told Stella all she needed to know. She smiled, took the ice cubes and hid them behind her back. In her most serious tone of voice, she yelled toward the rec room, "Grandmother says to get in here and help clean up this mess! You learn how to behave, Frankie!"

Frankie slowly walked in, eyes darting from Grandmother to Stella, but when he saw that the floor was clean, he stopped. He spun around to run, but Grandmother caught and held him while Stella pushed the ice cubes down his shirt! Albert had followed Frankie up the stairs and stood in the doorway, laughing. As Frankie whined, Grandmother gave him a playful slap on the behind. He ran away, into the basement. Albert and Stella remained.

All three of them stood together, holding themselves as they laughed in the fading afternoon sun. Soon they quieted and looked at each other. "Look at the strength in your sister," Grandmother said to Albert, "and obey her from now on." Stella stood straight as Albert promised.

Stella said, "Let's go teach him some things."

Looking at his sister with respect, Albert said, "Sure, Stella," and followed her. On the way down the stairs, she turned to him and said, "Just be yourself, Albert. You know what to do."

About Polychrome

Founded in 1990, Polychrome Publishing Corporation is an independent press located in Chicago, Illinois, producing children's books for a multicultural market. Polychrome books introduce characters and illustrate situations with which children of all colors can readily identify. They are designed to promote racial, ethnic, cultural and religious tolerance and understanding. We live in a multicultural world. We at Polychrome Publishing Corporation believe that our children need a balanced multicultural education if they are to thrive in that world. Polychrome books can help create that balance.

Acknowledgments

Polychrome Publishing Corporation appreciates the encouragement and help received from Christopher A. Chen, Michael and Kay Janis, Irene Cualoping, Gene Honda, Yvonne Lau, Ngoan Le, Rebecca Lederhouse, Lee Maglaya, Ashraf Manji, Gene Mayeda, Calvin Manshio and Peggy C. Wallace, Kyosik Oh, Sam and Harue Ozaki, Sandra R. Otaka, Lynn Watson, Philip Wong, Mitchell and Laura Witkowski, George and Vicki Yamate, Kiyo Yoshimura, and Kay Kawaguchi.

Other Books from Polychrome Publishing Corporation

Char Siu Bao Boy
ISBN 1-879965-00-3

Written by Sandra S. Yamate and illustrated by Joyce MW Jenkin, this story introduces us to Charlie, a Chinese American boy who loves eating his favorite ethnic food for lunch. His friends find his eating preferences strange. Charlie succumbs to peer pressure but misses eating his char siu bao. Find out how he learns to balance assimilation and cultural preservation. 32 pages hardbound (with color illustrations). *Recommended by the State of Hawaii Department of Education.*

Ashok By Any Other Name
ISBN 1-879965-01-1

Written by Sandra S. Yamate and illustrated by Janice Tohinaka. This story is about Ashok, an Indian American boy who wishes he had a more "American" name and the mishaps he experiences as he searches for the perfect name for himself. 36 pages hardbound with paper jacket (with color illustrations). *"The book is well-written and would make an excellent addition to a primary school library."* —*India West.*

Nene And The Horrible Math Monster
ISBN 1-879965-02-X

Written by Marie Villanueva and illustrated by Ria Unson. Nene, a Filipino American girl confronts the model minority myth, that all Asians excel at mathematics, and in doing so, overcomes her fears. 36 pages hardbound with paper jacket (with color illustrations). *"The book is engaging and delightful reading, not just for this age group [third grade], but for older school children, and adults as well."* —*Special Edition Press.*

Blue Jay In The Desert
ISBN 1-879965-04-6

Written by Marlene Shigekawa and illustrated by Isao Kikuchi. This is the story of a Japanese American boy and his family who are interned during World War II. It is the story of young Junior and his Grandfather's message of hope. 36 pages hardbound with paper jacket (with color illustrations).

ONE small GIRL
ISBN 1-879965-05-4

Written by Jennifer L. Chan and illustrated by Wendy K. Lee. Do all Asian Americans look alike? Jennifer Lee is one small girl trying to amuse herself in Grandmother's store and Uncle's store next door, but it's hard when she's not supposed to touch anything. As she goes back and forth between the two stores, Jennifer Lee finds a way to double the entertainment for one small girl in two big stores. 30 pages hardbound with paper jacket (with color illustrations).

Almond Cookies & Dragon Well Tea
ISBN 1-879965-03-8

Written by Cynthia Chin-Lee and illustrated by You Shan Tang. Erica, a European American girl, visits the home of Nancy, her Chinese American friend. In her glimpse of Nancy's cultural heritage, she finds much to admire and enjoy. Together, the two girls learn that the more they share, the more each of them has. 36 pages hardbound with paper jacket (with color illustrations). *"Well crafted. Very stylish for today's America."*—*The Book Reader.*

Thanksgiving At Obaachan's
ISBN 1-879965-07-0

Written and illustrated by Janet Mitsui Brown. A Japanese American girl describes the Thanksgiving celebration at her Grandmother's house and the things that make it her favorite holiday. 36 pages hardbound with paper jacket (with color illustrations).